Get Lavinia Goodbody!

By the same author:

Butterfingers
Grisel and the Tooth Fairy and Other Stories
Hanky-Panky
Paper Flags and Penny Ices
Sticky Fingers
Willy and the Semolina Pudding and Other Stories
Willy and the UFO and Other Stories

Get Lavinia Goodbody!

ROGER COLLINSON

Illustrated by JOHN SHELLEY

Andersen Press
London

First published in 1983 by
Andersen Press Limited,
20 Vauxhall Bridge Road, London SW1V 2SA
Reprinted 1985, 1995
www.andersenpress.co.uk

This edition first published in 2002

Text © 1983 by Roger Collinson
Illustrations © 1983 by John Shelley

The rights of Roger Collinson and John Shelley to be
identified as the author and illustrator of this work have
been asserted by them in accordance with the Copyright,
Designs and Patents Act, 1988.

British Library Cataloguing in Publication Data
available
ISBN 1 84270 097 9

Printed and bound in Great Britain by
the Guernsey Press Company Ltd., Guernsey,
Channel Islands

Contents

In all the woes that curse our race
There is a lady in the case.

W.S. Gilbert

1
The Hero's Return

This was the thirty-ninth time Figgy had run away from home. Now, you might suppose that he had cruel parents who beat him every day and starved him, but you would be wrong. Figgy wasn't often spanked, and you had only to glance at him to see that he did not go hungry. No, the truth is that whereas most people just slammed the door, or shouted, 'It ain't fair!', or cried, or wouldn't say 'Hello nicely', or took ten minutes to carry the dirty dishes to the sink, Figgy ran away from home.

But that's still not the whole truth. Figgy did *do* all those things – and he ran away from home as well.

'Where's Michael?' Figgy's dad would say.

'Oh, he's run away from home,' his mum would answer. 'Did you get that rice I wanted?'

Pretty cool, you say, for a mother whose little son had run away from home; but you must remember that if Figgy was always running off, he was always coming back. And, on each occasion, it was noted, he returned either at twelve-thirty or at five o'clock. Meals at Mrs Figg's house were very regular and very punctual. Figgy never ran away before his breakfast.

But this time, the thirty-ninth time, it would be

different. This time, there would be no turning back. With all the money he possessed tucked safely at the bottom of one pocket, Figgy strode towards the bus station. His intention? To board the first bus going out of town, buy a ticket to some far-off destination, and then trust himself to Fortune and his own resourcefulness. If they preferred Lavinia Goodbody to him, well then, they could have her!

The bus station was thronged with people who, finished with the weekend shopping, now only wanted to get back to their homes on the outskirts of Kirkston or in the villages beyond. Figgy found himself jostled by shoppers with their baskets and elbowed by mothers dragging children away from slot machines.

And then he spied a double-decker waiting with open doors. Without looking to see where the bus was going — it didn't really matter — Figgy climbed aboard and scrambled up the stairs, anxious to get a good seat at the front. To his delight, he had the top deck to himself, and sat gazing at the fretful crowds below.

Not long now and Kirkston would be left behind for ever. Not long now and they would all be saying, 'Where's Michael? . . . . Has anyone seen Michael?' And, when they realised he'd gone for good, then how would they feel? Rotten, he guessed — or at any rate, that's what he hoped.

So Mum thought it would be nice to have a girl

about the place! Well, if Mr and Mrs Goodbody were agreeable, she could have a girl about the place for good and all, for now there'd be a spare room — his room!

The first of the events which had led to this, Figgy's thirty-ninth attempt to run away, had occurred four or five weeks earlier when Mum and Dad had had a letter from Auntie Jane and Uncle Mick telling them that they had won five nights for two in Amsterdam (wherever that was). Figgy thought no more about it. Then, a few days later, came another letter, asking if Lavinia could come and stay. Auntie Jane and Uncle Mick said, of course, they could pay for a third place and take Lavinia with them, but they rather thought they'd like to make the trip a second honeymoon.

Figgy had not been thrilled by the prospect of having Lavinia in the house. Not that he knew much about her; he could remember seeing her only once, several years before, when she had been a bridesmaid at some wedding. But it was enough for Figgy that Lavinia was a girl.

Mum said, 'You're only a year younger than she is, Michael; it'll be someone for you to play with. You know how bored you get on holiday.'

And Peter chuckled, 'You never know, this might be the beginning of a great romance. If you want any tips, just ask big brother Pete.'

'You'll do no such thing!' Mum warned. 'And don't tease, Peter. You know what he's like when you start on at him.'

But that hadn't stopped Peter, every time they were on their own, reminding Figgy that it was now only so long before the Loverly Lavinia came, and wishing him sweet dreams. So, within a few days of her arrival, Figgy was already in a peevish mood.

And then Mum had announced calmly at the breakfast table that Figgy would have to move in and share with Peter to make room for Lavinia.

'But it's not fair!' protested Figgy. 'Why can't she have Peter's room?'

'Because your room's far too small for two. You boys would be at each other's throats in five minutes squeezed in there together. No, you can have a sleeping-bag on Peter's floor.'

'On the floor!' Figgy almost screamed.

'Michael, don't make a scene,' said Mrs Figg. 'When we went to stay at Grandma's you know you begged to be the one who had the sleeping-bag.'

This was true; but there seemed to Figgy, at that moment, to be a world of difference between camping out in Grandma's front room on Christmas Eve and being told you were to sleep for a week on the floor in your own house so that a strange girl could have *your* bed in *your* room.

'It's not fair!' he repeated. 'And what about my

things? She'll be interfering with all my things.'

'Little girls,' said Mrs Figg, 'are not likely to be interested in your collection of football cards, half-finished models of aeroplanes, heaps of grubby comics, jars of stick insects, chemistry sets, and . . . and goodness knows what else!'

'But she'll . . . .'

'And if there's anything so precious, so precious that you think a well brought-up young lady will steal or damage it, you can take it with you into Peter's room.'

'I'm not having his old junk in my room!' Peter snapped.

For the next three days, Figgy sulked, and he and Peter could not meet without an argument.

Lavinia was to arrive by the afternoon train on Saturday, and Mr Figg would meet her while Mrs Figg prepared the tea. At dinner time she suggested that it would be nice if the boys went with their father.

'Can't,' said Peter. 'Got a training session with the Under-Sixteens squad.'

'What? In the holiday?' said Mrs Figg. 'Well, Michael, you're not doing anything, and you like collecting train numbers.'

'No, I don't! If he's not going, I'm not!'

And nothing could persuade Figgy to greet his cousin at the station.

'I don't know what's got into you,' Mrs Figg declared. 'All I can say is I'm looking forward to having a nice little girl about the place. I've had just about enough of boys!'

It was then that Figgy had decided he would run away and not come back.

Running away usually meant going to the park or down along the river bank. Figgy had never before got on a bus heading for the great unknown, and, now that he had taken this desperate step, he was impatient to be on his way.

Sitting on your own, waiting, especially waiting for an adventure, is something which does not agree with many people. What seemed exciting shrinks, little by little, like a bright balloon, until nothing's left except an uneasy feeling in your stomach and a wish that you were back again with the people and the things you know.

Figgy found that he was thinking anxiously about where he was to sleep that night. Hedgerows and haystacks, he knew from stories he had read, were the regular lodgings of heroes when they set out on their adventures; but, as he tried to picture himself in the dark, alone with only mice and beetles and . . . and *things* for company, he began to question if adventures were quite the fun that story books had led him to believe. A sleeping-bag in Peter's room, the front door locked and bolted, the light left burning on the landing: how cosy and secure they were! And tramps!

What about tramps? Was it possible that he could end up as one of those boys you hear about who disappear? Figgy imagined Mum and Dad on television, tearfully explaining when their son had last been seen. He swallowed the lump that bobbed up in his throat and pulled himself together. Serve them right if he was never found again. Perhaps they'd wish then they hadn't turned him out to make room for their Lavinia.

The commotion of a family climbing on the bus broke in upon his thoughts. The children came clattering up the stairs, while their parents, burdened with the week's provisions, laboured after them. On seeing Figgy already in possession of the front seat, the boy and girl fell silent for a moment; then, 'Come on!' said the boy. 'Let's go down the back.'

'Oh no, you don't!' his mother panted, as her crimson face popped up like Judy after Mr Punch. 'We've come upstairs to please you, but we're not traipsing all the way back there.' So saying, she sank down upon the nearest seat.

'Do as your mother says,' her husband added, and occupied the seat behind his wife with bags and parcels heaped beside him.

Figgy no longer felt at ease at the front there by himself, thinking that he was being looked at by four pairs of curious eyes.

He need not have worried. He was of no interest to the man and woman, who were conducting a one-sided conversation about prices, the heat, next door's cat, and a certain Mrs Foskett. The children pointed at things outside, fidgeted and argued.

'. . . I thought when Beryl comes to tea tomorrow,' said their mother, 'I'd do one of my blackcurrant flans; I've got a tub of double cream.'

A tub of double cream.

Like an alarm clock, the words rang in Figgy's memory. He remembered Mum putting double cream down on her shopping list; he remembered Mum saying she'd make a trifle as a special treat for when Lavinia came. And Mum's trifles were the last word in deliciousness, with the sponge soaked in jelly, the fruit and·the nuts, the custard and the cream, and the little chocolate drops sprinkled on the top. Trifles appeared on the tea table only for Christmas and birthdays and important visitors.

Figgy's mouth watered, and he realised that he was feeling hungry. And where was his next meal coming from? He'd have no money left. And how do you find anything to eat when you've run away from home? He should have brought a packed meal with him: some bread and cheese and crisps and biscuits — but no *trifle!* And there wouldn't be any of it left. Peter would see to that — the pig! — delighted that Figgy wasn't home to eat his share. It wasn't fair!

Figgy turned and spoke to the man and woman.

'Excuse me. Please, have you got the time?'

At first they didn't hear, and he had to ask again.

'He wants to know the time,' the woman told her husband.

'It's about half-past four,' he said. 'We should be off any minute now.'

Figgy hadn't long to make his mind up. If he hurried, he could just get home for tea. Have his trifle and make better plans to run away tomorrow. Yes, that's what he'd do.

And at that moment, the bus shuddered into noisy motion. The bell clanged, and, to Figgy's open-mouthed dismay, they were already swinging out of the bus station, into the main road leading out of town. He watched, too taken aback to move, as shops and banks and offices rushed by. Down one hill, through the traffic lights, a change of gear, and they were roaring up the other side, on the road to who knew where.

At last, Figgy struggled to his feet and was lurching down the stairs just as the conductor came climbing up.

Now, the conductor was not a man who cared for little boys — too many bad experiences of hordes of school children had left him bitter and suspicious, and he had no intention of giving way to Figgy, who retreated up the stairs butted by the conductor's global belly.

'P-please,' Figgy stammered, 'please, I want to get off.'

'Hasn't no one ever told you how to behave on a

bus?' the conductor asked. 'Kids!' he said — he
addressed the man and woman over Figgy's head —
'You'd think the parents would teach them manners.
But they don't, not half of them.'

The man and woman tutted their agreement, while
their children gazed at Figgy wondering what he could
have done.

'Please, I've got to get off!' Figgy pleaded.

Without looking, the conductor raised an arm and
jabbed the bell-push. At the same time, he twirled the

handle of his machine and held a ticket under Figgy's nose.

'25p,' he said.

'What?' said Figgy.

'You heard. 25p. From the bus station, half-fare, 25p.'

'But it's a mistake,' said Figgy. 'I didn't want to come.'

'Ooh!' exclaimed the woman. 'Don't tell stories! You was sitting there when we came up, and you asked my husband what time the bus went.'

'See what I mean?' said the conductor with a sniff. 'They're up to all the dodges, I can tell you .... Now, 25p, or I'll call a policeman.'

Figgy pulled the money from his pocket. The bus drew up, and he escaped.

Figgy had not been travelling on the bus for more than a few minutes, but, when he got off, it seemed that he had been carried miles away. He turned and hurried back, angry and almost tearful. What a mess he'd made of everything! 25p wasted. Not running *away* but running *home*. And certain now to be late in getting back for tea. That wouldn't please Mum, and it would mean explanations. He tried to think of a convincing lie. Getting lost? .... What, in Kirkston! .... Being kidnapped? .... Dad wasn't rich enough to pay a ransom .... How about losing his memory? .... Figgy had heard of people who lost their memories, didn't know who they were or where they lived. He could say he'd found himself on the other side of town and couldn't remember how he'd got there. Well, it was worth a try.

He dodged and edged his way along the pavements. Everyone was hurrying the other way or wandered two and three abreast as if no one in the world could have a mother waiting for him or was going to miss his share of trifle.

At last, he turned the corner into Stanley Road. Another minute and he had come to Number 17. Figgy slipped round the side way to the back — family never used the front. The kitchen door was open, and he could hear voices in happy conversation: Mum and Dad and, sometimes, even Peter. He peeped through the window and saw them standing there, their backs to him as they chatted with the visitor.

2
'I'm Sorry Now I Wrote It'

Lavinia Goodbody sat on one of the high kitchen stools, smiling at her aunt, her uncle and her older cousin. Unlike Figgy's memory of the little bridesmaid, Lavinia was now a tall girl, with shining chestnut hair. She was dressed in brown dungarees, a T-shirt and trainers. She might be still eleven, but she could have passed for thirteen anywhere.

'I can't think where Michael's got to,' Mrs Figg was saying. 'It's not like Michael to be late for tea.'

'Is that him?' asked Lavinia. 'Peeping at us through the window?'

Too late Figgy ducked.

'Michael!' his mother called. 'Whatever are you doing? Come in here and meet Lavinia.'

It was every bit as bad as Figgy had always known it would be. Here he was, turned out of his room for Lavinia's sake, and the first thing she did was to make him look a fool. But there was nothing for it but to go in and be polite — as polite as he could manage.

'Here's your cousin,' said Mrs Figg. 'Say hello.'

'Hello,' Figgy said.

'Hello,' said Lavinia, smiling down at him. 'Auntie says you're going to let me have your room.'

Peter caught Figgy's eye and smirked.

Mrs Figg caught Figgy's eye: her own was steely with its warning.

'Lavinia's train was late,' said Mr Figg. 'We've only just got back.'

'Yes, you must be starving, love,' said Mrs Figg. 'It's long past tea time. We'll just take your things upstairs and then I'll put the kettle on. Peter, take Lavinia's case and show her where to go.'

'No!' cried Figgy. 'Let me do it.'

'But Lavinia's case is heavy,' said Mrs Figg, bewildered by his offer. 'Better let Peter manage it.'

'No!' Figgy almost shouted. 'I want to do it. I can . . . I can show her where things are.'

'Well, all right, dear . . . if you're sure.' She struggled hard to understand what had brought about this sudden change, and forced a breathy laugh. 'I can see you two are going to get on famously.'

Panic!

It was sheer panic that got Figgy up the stairs — Lavinia's case and all — with the speed and strength that only panic can afford. It was a miracle that Mrs Figg had not already found it. Frantically, he fumbled with his door, flung it open and fell into the room.

Without rising from his knees, he stretched clawing fingers to his bedside table. He scarcely saw but felt the note, and thrust it down inside his jeans. Then, trembling with relief, he lay panting on the floor.

It had not been until Mum had asked Peter to see Lavinia to his room that Figgy had remembered. How he had forgotten Figgy never could explain. But, for whatever reason, he had forgotten the note he'd left behind him when he ran away that afternoon.

Now, if that note had merely stated the bald facts of his running away, it would not have mattered much. The family knew he didn't care for the arrangements for his cousin's visit. But Figgy hadn't been content with just the simple facts.

When you are running away forever, you may feel free to write things you would never dare to write if you thought you would ever have to meet those people face to face again.

And Figgy had written *things*.

Especially things about Lavinia. Things too terrible to be printed in a book. References to certain farmyard animals were included in the milder passages. And there were two whole sides of writing — quite the longest composition he had ever done.

'Are you all right, Michael?'

Lavinia had followed him, and now stood in the doorway, looking down on him once more.

''Course,' he said. 'Just tripped.'

'Whatever's happened? What's he gone and done?'

It was Mrs Figg, hurrying up the stairs with Mr Figg and Peter hard upon her heels to see what all the noise was.

'Showing off!' said Mum. 'Trying to look big. I told you that case was too heavy for you.'

Peter sniggered. 'Just as well it wasn't Lavinia he was carrying.'

Mr Figg smothered a chuckle with a cough, while Figgy glared at Peter.

The tea table was spread with an abundant feast: best ham salad, jam sponge, fruit cake, meringues, and, in pride of place, the celebration trifle. The 'men' gave their attention, for the most part, to emptying their plates, leaving Mrs Figg to entertain Lavinia.

'. . . And you've got your silver medal now for swimming, have you? I think that's wonderful. Our Peter's like a fish in water, but Michael's not got both feet off the bottom yet . . . . Horse riding! Well, I never! You don't go jumping over fences, do you? . . . . And ballet dancing! Oh, that's lovely! I sometimes wish one of mine had been a little girl so she could have gone to ballet . . . . You've got *boys* in your ballet class! Still, I can't see our Michael in a pair of tights . . . . And you've just got another certificate for the violin! Congratulations! I noticed your violin case. You'll have to give us all a tune . . . . Of course you can do your practice every day. You haven't reached your standard without working at it. I keep telling Michael, if you want to make a go of something, you've just got

to keep on work, work, working at it all the time.'

Was there no end to Lavinia's talents and achievements? Even his father was looking weary of the subject, Figgy thought. And the only way he could keep himself from groaning aloud was to fix his mind firmly on the trifle.

At last, Mrs Figg helped everybody to a share. The suck and squelch as she scooped the mixture from the bowl, the flop as it fell into the waiting dish and lay there moist, richly textured, colourful — this pleasured ears, eyes, nose and imagination all before' the first spoonful had fulfilled its promise on the tongue. This made up for everything — well, very nearly. But whether to eat fast or slowly? Always a problem when it came to trifle. On the one hand, you wanted to prolong the treat; after all, it could be months before the trifle bowl appeared again. On the other, if there was a chance of second helpings and Peter finished first . . . . Then it occurred to Figgy that today, of course, it would be Lavinia who got the last scrapings as she was 'visitors'. So, comforting himself with the thought that without Lavinia there would have been no trifle, he settled down to make his portion last.

'Now, Lavinia,' said Mrs Figg, 'I'm sure you could manage just another mouthful.'

'It's delicious, Auntie,' said Lavinia, 'but I won't have any more.'

Figgy could not believe his ears, but gobbled what

he'd been so carefully saving, just in case they hadn't played him false.

'Oh, come now, dear,' said Mrs Figg. 'There's just a taster left.'

'No, really, Auntie, I won't have any more. I'm sure Michael would be glad of it. Little boys can never have enough.'

Figgy almost choked. 'Little boys! . . . . *Little* boys!' Who did she think she was? One year older, that was all! And she needn't keep on about how short he was. '*Little boys*!' She sounded like a grown-up or a teacher. The cheek! The fantastic, unheard-of, unpardonable *cheek*!

'You're quite right, my dear,' said Mrs Figg. 'If they gave medals for eating, I think Michael would get the gold.'

Figgy did not join in the laughter, and, when Mrs Figg offered him the left-overs from the trifle, he declined them coldly.

'Well, I've heard everything!' said Mrs Figg.

'I'll have it, Mum,' said Peter.

After tea, Mrs Figg suggested that a quiet game of Scrabble or Monopoly would be a good idea, bearing in mind that Lavinia had had a tiring journey. Tomorrow the boys would show her all the sights of Kirkston.

When Figgy found that he had mortgaged all his

25

properties and still owed Lavinia fifteen hundred pounds, he announced that he was going up to bed. Peter said he was going to meet some friends down at the youth club and went upstairs with him to change. It was only recently he'd taken to changing for visits to the club, and, though he had no need to shave, he kept some after-shave hidden in his cupboard and patted it about his face.

Figgy kicked the sleeping-bag spread out at the foot of Peter's bed and sullenly began undressing. Then, as he pulled his jeans off, the note he'd so desperately stuffed down the front fell out, and Peter pounced on it.

'Hey, hey! What's this?' he cried, holding it above his head.

'Give it here!' hissed Figgy, snatching at it, but hindered by the trousers round his ankles.

'Notes to the Loverly Lavinia is it? Better let me have a look, just to check your spelling.'

'Give it me!' Figgy raged, and hurled himself at Peter.

One-handed, Peter overcame him, and sat on Figgy's chest, his arms pinned helplessly beneath his knees.

'And now,' he said, unfolding the note, 'we shall see what we shall see.' For a moment or two he read in silence. Then he whistled. 'Well, well, well, Master Figg! So *that's* what Lavinia is! I never would have guessed to look at her. It's not the usual thing to call your sweetheart.'

'She ain't my sweetheart!'

'Nor never likely to be, if she gets to hear of this. *Hello*! Something about *me*? ". . . And Peter is a smelly toe-rag." Oh, I am, am I?'

'Yes,' puffed Figgy. 'A stinking, smelly toe-rag!'

'I don't know how you've got the nerve,' said Peter. He leaned back and pulled off one of Figgy's socks. 'When it comes to smelly toe-rags, this is enough to make other decent, well brought-up feet pass out. *Cor*! To think I've got to sleep in the same room as these! Here, have a sniff! It's yours!' And Peter dangled the sweaty sock under Figgy's nose.

Figgy bucked and squirmed, but Peter was too heavy for him.

'Now, the question is,' said Peter, holding up the note, 'what are we going to do with this?'

'Give it me!' said Figgy.

'Oh, no! Oh, dear me, no! That would never do. Why, you might get rid of it, and what use would it be then? If you got rid of it, Mum couldn't see it; Dad couldn't see it; the Loverly Lavinia couldn't see it. No, I think it would be best if I looked after it, just to make sure it doesn't come to any harm. And, of course, to make sure *you* don't come to any harm.'

'What d'you mean?' snapped Figgy.

'Well, if Mum or Dad did find this interesting document, I wouldn't like to be in your pants — or, rather, *not* in your pants. Remember the last time? — When you "borrowed" Mum's fur coat to play Abominable Snowmen? Very sore about the seat you were; almost as red as your horrid little face is now.'

Figgy did remember. He could not forget the stinging slaps, and winced. Not many crimes were spankable with Mrs Figg, but, when she spanked, she meant it. Down with the trousers, across her knees — and wallop! The note would, beyond all doubt, be spanking business.

'Of course,' said Peter, 'if I'm going to look after you, you'll want to show your gratitude.'

'What d'you mean?' growled Figgy.

'Well, if I ask you to do any little thing for me, of course you'll do it.'

'Like what?'

'Oh, I don't know,' said Peter wearily. 'But there are bound to be umpteen jobs a bright and willing boy like you can do. Well, for a start, I don't really think I want to ˙waste my time tomorrow trailing the Loverly Lavinia round Kirkston; so, instead of kicking up a fuss, you'll make it plain you'd much rather take your cousin out all by yourself.'

'I won't! It's not . . . .'

Peter waved the note before his eyes.

'. . . Not fair? Is that what you meant to say? Well, the choice is yours: a little walk with Lavinia, or . . . Need I say more?'

'That's . . . that's *blackmail!*' cried Figgy.

'You've been watching too much telly,' Peter said. 'Well, are you going to be sensible?'

He bounced up and down until Figgy breathlessly agreed.

Peter got up, and Figgy watched him as he pulled on his best jeans, watched him comb his hair, watched him as he put the note carefully inside the zip-pocket of his denim jacket. At the door, Peter turned and said: 'This note of yours, about running away.'

'Well?'

'Why did you bother to come back?'

3
Insult and Injury

On Sundays, the Figgs had what they called 'a bit of a lay-in'. No one had to get up for work or school; no alarm clocks were set, and everyone snoozed on undisturbed.

Figgy himself was as good a snoozer as any of them. He was the first to stir now only because he had managed to roll in the sleeping-bag so that his head was pushed against the foot of Peter's bed. He woke, half dreaming he was tied up and locked in a narrow dungeon, and, when his eyes opened, he could not, for a moment, understand where he was. Then he remembered everything, especially the note and how Peter had threatened to make use of it. He had to get that note back.

Figgy listened hard. No one was moving, and there was no sound from Peter except for his heavy breathing. Silently, like a little maggot, Figgy wriggled from the sleeping-bag. Where should he look first? Peter's jeans and jacket lay on the floor where he had pulled them off when he had come in the night before. Nervously, Figgy undid the zip of the jacket pocket and his fingers searched for the folded sheet of paper. But there was no note, nothing. He tried the other pockets

— only a comb. Then he seized the jeans — a grubby handkerchief and thirty pence.

Where had Peter hidden it? Figgy's eyes skidded from the bookshelf, to the carpet, to the sportsbag. He decided to try Peter's other clothes and opened the wardrobe door. Figgy knew it squeaked but not as noisily as that. He was rummaging through faded jeans and outgrown jackets, trying not to rattle the wire hangers, when Peter spoke.

'This what you're looking for, you little creep?'

Peter, leaning on one elbow, waved the note temptingly at Figgy. His voice, shattering the guilty silence, made Figgy leap into the air.

'You don't think, do you,' said Peter, 'that I'd leave this where sneaky little kids could nick it?'

'I like that!' said Figgy. 'You nicked it from me!'

'I'm glad you like it,' said Peter. 'That means we're both happy. And now, before you say anything I might have to bash you for, I think I'd like a mug of tea. Two spoons of sugar.'

'Well, you can just . . . .'

'Oh no, I can't,' said Peter. 'Remember, we have an agreement. *I* make sure no one else sees this, and you, *you* do little things for me. Like making me a cup of tea.'

Figgy was beaten and he turned to go.

'And one thing more,' said Peter.

'What?'

'On your way down, look in on the Loverly Lavinia

and see if she could drink one too.'

Figgy gaped in disbelief.

'Go on,' said Peter. 'I'll be listening. So be sure you ask her ... and, Figgy ....'

'What?'

' ... ask her nicely.'

The door to Figgy's room, as always, stood ajar, it not being possible to close it. Fixing the door to Figgy's room had been an item on a list of jobs for Mr Figg ever since they had moved into the house seven years ago.

Figgy poked his head into the room. Lavinia was still sleeping. Beside her on the pillow a fluffy pink teddy bear stared glassily at the Airfix planes that hung on cottons from the ceiling. Folded neatly on the chair were Lavinia's clothes, and several paperbacks were stacked squarely on the chest-of-drawers next to a photograph of Auntie Jane and Uncle Mick inscribed with 'To Our Little Flower, from Mumsie and Daddo'.

Figgy returned to Peter's room.

'She's asleep,' he hissed.

'Then wake her up,' said Peter.

'How?'

'How did the Prince wake Sleeping Beauty?'

'Eh?' Figgy grunted, slow to see what fairy stories had to do with Lavinia. 'Well, he ....' The answer to Peter's question froze upon his lips. 'No!' he whispered vehemently. 'I won't!' And he was gone before Peter could threaten him again.

Lavinia was still sleeping when Figgy's head tortoised between the door frame and the door; but before he could decide whether to cough or whistle, she stirred and her eyes opened.

'Hello,' she said. 'What time is it?'

'Dunno.'

'I'm not late, am I? I mean, I'm not the last one up?'

'No, I'm the only one who's up.'

'After worms?'

Figgy did not understand. Did she think he was going fishing? Or was she making fun of him? He rather thought she was.

'What d'you mean?'

'Early bird catches the worm,' Lavinia said. 'You being first up. You know.'

'What about my tea?' called Peter. 'And don't forget you-know-what.'

'What's that?' Lavinia asked.

'I'm making tea,' Figgy mumbled. 'Do you want some?'

Lavinia beamed.

'I'd love some. Two sugars, please.'

At the breakfast table, Mrs Figg declared, 'Wonders will never cease! Fancy Michael getting up to make the tea! You must be a wonderful influence on him, Lavinia dear. If he's like this when you've not been in the house five minutes, so to speak, what will he be like before you leave?'

'Unbelievable!' said Mr Figg, fixing his younger son with a suspicious eye.

'I've said it before . . .' Mrs Figg began.

'Five times, to be precise,' Peter interrupted her. 'But don't let me stop you saying it again.'

'And don't you be so cheeky,' said Mrs Figg. 'It's not often I have reason to praise our Michael, but, credit where credit's due, that's what I say.'

'Don't you think I deserve some credit for Michael's good deed for the day?' said Peter. 'I'm sure Michael does.'

Peter grinned at Figgy and patted the pocket of his denim jacket where Figgy knew the note was safely zipped away.

'Now,' said Mrs Figg, 'if you two boys take Lavinia out and show her the sights, I'll get on with the dinner.'

'Sorry,' Peter said. 'I can't. I arranged to meet Nigs and Darren. But I'm sure Michael won't mind looking after Lavinia on his own. The park would be nice this morning.'

Figgy knew why Peter had suggested this. He met his mates there most Sunday mornings and Peter guessed Figgy wouldn't want them to see him with Lavinia.

But Mrs Figg agreed with Peter. The park was nice. Quite like being in the country. And there were swings and things to go on, so long as you weren't wearing clothes that could be spoilt. Had Lavinia brought any old clothes with her?

'These are my old clothes, Auntie,' said Lavinia, glancing at her crisp, white T-shirt and spotless jeans. 'And it wouldn't take me five minutes to rinse them through and iron them if they did get grubby.'

'You never do your own washing, Lavinia!' gasped Mrs Figg.

'Oh, quite often, things like that. Mummy believes children should learn independence.'

'I should have had girls,' said Mrs Figg. 'Independence! Michael can't be trusted to wash his neck, let alone his shirts — and you're no better, Peter!'

The sun that sparkled down on Kirkston could not dispel the gloom that hovered over Figgy's head. He did not talk to Lavinia, beyond grunting an answer to her questions. Whether she put this down to the sulks or to his being shy, he didn't know and he didn't care.

The park was on a hillside and when the snow fell was a great attraction to all the young people of Kirkston, who slid and tumbled down its slopes on toboggans, tin trays and even skis. It was less suitable for football, though there were those who argued that lads who had learned to control a ball on the park pitches were at an advantage when playing matches on the level.

Today the grass was sprinkled with boys punting balls among themselves and shooting at goals marked out by shirts and sweaters.

Inside the gates, Figgy stood and looked about him. He spotted the group he was searching for, and, with a sigh and a muttered 'this way' to Lavinia, he plodded dejectedly towards it.

'Shoot!' screamed a ginger boy in glasses, as another, a beefy boy, booted the ball with great ferocity in the direction of the goal. The keeper dived with dramatic style, missed the ball by yards, and then lay panting on the ground waiting for applause.

'Goal!' bellowed the beefy boy, running and leaping with fists raised above his head.

'Goal!' roared the bespectacled boy.

36

'Goal! Great goal!' howled a third, who sprang on the scorer to give him the victor's hug.

'No, it weren't!' squealed the goalkeeper, still sprawling.

"Course it was!' shouted the beefy boy.

'No, it weren't!'

'You calling me a liar?'

'No,' the goalkeeper replied more quietly. 'But it weren't a goal.'

'I ask you. Weren't that a goal?' The beefy boy turned to his team mates.

'Yeah!' sniffed a boy with a running nose, known to everyone outside his family as Snotts. 'It sort of came along like this, and curled round the post sort of like this, sort of.' With his hand he traced a flight path so erratic that the ball appeared to have been radio-controlled.

'No, it never!' cried the goalkeeper, scrambling to his feet. 'It went sort of like this.' And his hand followed a route that took the ball twisting round the other side of the imaginary post. He looked back to plead his cause and noticed Figgy. "Ere, did you see it, Figgy?'

'Yeah.'

'Well, I ask you, was that a goal?'

'Yeah, it was,' said Figgy.

'See!' jeered the ginger boy with glasses. 'Told yer!'

'Oh, shut up, Gogsie!' the goalkeeper shouted. He sat down heavily with his back to them and began scratching at his arm-pits. This habit had earned him the nickname Scratcher, and, on three occasions the school nurse had examined him from head to toe but had discovered nothing that ought not to have been there. He was, it seemed, just an itchy boy. And when and where he itched, then and there he scratched.

'You're late,' said the beefy boy. 'Who's she?'

All the boys, apart from Scratcher, now tearing at a spot between his shoulder blades, stared at Lavinia. No one knew what to make of this girl standing quietly at Figgy's side. Not even Basher had got round to girlfriends yet, but the alarming thought whispered to him now that that little titch, Figgy, had beaten him to something. Basher had always to be the first or the best, and he was careful to choose friends he could be sure of beating. For a start, he was the oldest and the biggest, the best at football, the fastest runner; had most pocket money, the most flashy bike; and, if anyone ever dared to challenge him, he could punch and kick the hardest. He did not actually *know* more bad words than the others, but he did dare *use* more than the others dared, except when they were in their den and nobody could hear them. Occasionally, he stole a cigarette and he puffed at it looking very big, and no one guessed it made him feel sick and that he much preferred mint toffees. But, if this girl were Figgy's 'bird', it would be a blow to Basher's standing. It wouldn't have been so bad if she had been skinny or spotty or wore glasses. But this girl was all right. Basher decided quickly that he had better make the idea of Figgy and a girlfriend sound ridiculous, so he repeated, 'Who's she then?' and added, laughing like a car with a flat battery, 'Your bird?'

The laughter and the 'bird' were a signal to Snotts and Gogsie, who obediently made laughing noises too.

'She your bird then?' Basher said again.

'No, she ain't!' snapped Figgy. 'She's me cousin.'

'Your *cousin*!' Basher shrieked. 'He says she's his cousin!' And he staggered about, laughing as if Figgy had said Lavinia was his pet brontosaurus.

The others, deciding that 'cousin' was a thousand times more comical than 'bird', rolled on the ground.

'And what's her name?' gasped Basher.

Lavinia, who had been regarding this display with the cool interest of a scientist studying the antics of a band of apes, replied, 'Her name's Lavinia. What's yours?'

Basher ignored her question. He would have felt pretty silly introducing himself as Basher to a stranger who was clearly not at all impressed. He did not answer her, but found another subject for his wit.

'Lav!' he practically screamed. 'Lav! . . . 'Ere, boys, Figgy's cousin — her name's *Lav!*'

' . . . inia,' Lavinia corrected him. 'But still you haven't told me your name.'

'He knows,' said Basher, switching off his laugh. He

nodded at Figgy. 'He knows; ask him.'

This was a mistake. Basher was expecting Figgy to announce his nickname; and, at any other time, that is what Figgy would have done. But, today, Basher had misjudged him. From the very first, of course, he had offended Figgy; he had intended to. But in making fun of Lavinia's name he had gone too far. Not that Figgy didn't think it funny — he did that all right; and 'Lav' from now on was what he'd call Lavinia — to himself, at least. Basher's mistake was in making fun of Figgy's *cousin's* name. It was worse than making fun of Figgy's own. So, when Basher said, 'He knows; ask him', he did not expect Figgy to come out with the name that was entered in the register at school, the name the vicar had given him when he was christened, the name his mother and his father and relations used.

'Archibald,' said Figgy. 'His name's Archibald.'

Scratcher, Snotts and Gogsie had known for years that Basher's name was Archibald. But they still found it funny, and had to smother their giggles when they heard Figgy come right out with it. 'Lavinia' was unusual and a girl's name, but 'Archibald' was soppy.

Strangers always wondered how a plain Kirkston lad came to be stuck with it. The answer was a wealthy Scottish grandfather of that name, and Basher's parents hoped that some of his wealth would come their way if they named their first son in honour of the ancient Archibald. The infant Archibald had not been consulted, and, by the time he was old enough to protest about it, it was already six or seven years too late.

The risk Figgy had taken in uttering this name in public was terrible. Blood had stained the playground more than once when a reckless boy had dared to taunt Basher with his 'Archibald'.

But Figgy had risked more than being bashed when he exposed the bully's weak spot; for Basher, Gogsie, Snotts and Scratcher were more than friends — they were a Gang. The Gang did nothing in particular; it didn't have a secret password or a fancy name. And the chief attraction of belonging to the Gang was that everybody else did *not* belong, *could* not belong, because you could only join if the other members let you.

In fact, Figgy was the only other boy who wanted to. For some weeks they had let him tag along with them for games of football in the playground or the park. But he was not a member, and he'd not been taken to their secret hide-out.

Figgy had got Gogsie on his own one day and asked him.

'Do you think Basher would have me?'

'Dunno,' said Gogsie. 'But I'll tell him, and there'll have to be a Gang meeting about it. Of course, we don't let many join.'

The discussion had been a long one.

'Bit of a Mummy's boy, ain't he?' said Snotts,

sniffing at a candle. 'I mean, he's a bit posh.'

'No, he ain't,' said Scratcher. 'Most people keep a hanky in their pocket.'

'He's not much good at football,' Basher said.

'But he's keen,' said Gogsie, 'and you could learn him.'

In the end, they all voted to let Figgy join, all except Snotts, who kept on saying Figgy was a bit too posh. Figgy would have to pass the test, of course; all new members had to. And it had been decided to tell Figgy this Sunday in the park. But had Figgy made Basher change his mind?

Surprise had got the better of him for a moment, and then Lavinia asked without a smile, 'What name do your friends use?' Lavinia could have teased him; she could have got her own back. Basher knew it; the others knew it; Lavinia knew it well. But all she said was, 'What name do your friends use?'

Basher kicked the ground and spat before he told her.

'Basher.'

'Oh,' said Lavinia. 'Do you do a lot of bashing?'

Basher only shrugged his shoulders in answer to Lavinia, turned and began to dribble the ball round Scratcher who was still sitting on the ground.

'Come on — let's get on with it!'

Snotts and Gogsie galloped after him. Figgy lingered by Lavinia, not sure if he was meant to play, until the

42

ball rolled to his feet and he passed it on to Basher.

'Thanks. Nice one!' Basher panted generously, as he charged once more towards the goal and shot for all that he was worth at Scratcher. The ball soared into the air like a drop-kick in rugby. There was no question this time of its being a goal, but the sheer power and height won Basher enough applause to keep him cheerful.

'Blimey! I thought it was going into orbit, Basher!'

'Good job Scratcher didn't stop that one; it would've flattened him.'

Scratcher collected the ball and added his tribute, tossing the ball from hand to hand and laughing, "Ere, it's red 'ot. You feel it.'

The game went on its noisy, wild and clumsy way. Lavinia stood by, neglected.

At last they all sprawled on the grass and gossiped. Basher seemed as friendly and good-humoured as he ever was, lying full-length and chewing at a blade of grass, and Figgy thought that this would be as good a time as any to try his luck.

'Basher?'

'Yeah?'

'Did Gogsie tell you I want to join the Gang?'

'Yeah.'

'Well, can I . . . join?'

Basher raised his head and spat expertly at a daisy.

'Can I, Basher?'

Basher blew down his nose and pulled thoughtfully at an earlobe.

'Oh, go on, Basher — please.'

'Well, Figgy, you're a bit young.'

'I'm only one class behind you.'

'As I was saying, you're a bit young and there ain't much of you. I mean, you wouldn't be much use in a bundle.'

'I'd be as much use as Gogsie; he never fights 'cause of his glasses.'

'That ain't true,' protested Gogsie.

'Yes it is,' said Basher. 'So shut your face.'

'You know my mum won't let me take 'em off.'

'Shut it!' Basher said again.

'Well, can I, Basher?' Figgy pressed him.

'Yeah, all right then.'

'Thanks, Basher.'

'You've still got to do the test.'

'Oh.'

'Meet Gogsie after tea, tonight.'

'Where?'

'Corner of Wellington Street. He'll bring you to the hide-out.'

'Why me?' Gogsie muttered.

''Cos I say,' said Basher.

Lavinia, without waiting longer for an invitation, strolled over to the boys and tapped the football with her toe.

'Do you mind if I play with this for a few minutes?'

'Help yourself,' said Basher, with a smile as warm as cracking ice. 'It's a football,' he added. 'You kick it.'

The Gang looked on, curious to see what a girl — and a girl with the name Lavinia — would get up to with a football. Their curiosity became astonishment.

The ball seemed to twinkle at Lavinia's feet as she danced with it here and there, about the gaping boys. Deftly she controlled it, now with the inside of the foot and now the outside, turning and heeling to outwit an imaginary tackle. Then she kept the ball in the air, first by bouncing it on her insteps, then on her knees. Her display ended when she kicked the ball up and caught and balanced it between her head and shoulders.

The boys gazed silently, then turned to Basher.

'Huh!' he scoffed, standing up. 'All very fancy. But it wouldn't be much good in a real game. Wouldn't have the power to shoot hard. Not like *this*.' Lavinia had lightly punted the ball to him and it lay at his feet. Without a word of warning, Basher kicked it savagely. The ball flew towards Lavinia; but, without flinching, she trapped it, brought it down, and sent it hurtling back at Basher. When the ball struck him in the stomach, he was unprepared. Winded and speechless, he dropped down to his knees. The Gang stood round him in embarrassed silence.

'Come on, Michael,' said Lavinia. 'It's getting on for lunch time. Auntie will be expecting us.' And she turned to go.

'*Lunch!*' Snotts mimicked her. 'If you don't reckon Figgy's posh, she bloomin' is!'

'Oh, shut up!' said Figgy.

'Better get along,' said Scratcher. 'Lavinia will be cross.'

'I'm sorry, Basher,' Figgy said. 'I can still come tonight, can't I? For the test? Please, Basher.'

Basher's eyes followed Lavinia as she walked away, and the light which burned in them was cold and vengeful.

'Yeah, you come, Figgy,' he replied. 'You make sure you come.'

4

Get Lavinia Goodbody!

Figgy caught up with Lavinia and walked beside her.
She said nothing, and, at last, Figgy's curiosity got the
better of him.

'Where'd you learn all that then?'

'All what?' she said.

'You know — all *that.*'

'Oh, *that?*'

'Yes.'

'It's all part of general ball skills at my school,' said
Lavinia. 'Our teachers say girls have feet just the same
as boys, so they ought to learn to use them.'

If the girls at Lavinia's school were all as good as
that, what must their boys be like? Figgy was very
thoughtful. It would be great to be able to do some of
those things. Perhaps Lavinia would give him some
practice.... As soon as he realised what he was
thinking, Figgy stopped himself. Ask that stuck-up,
show-off girl to teach him football! Not bloomin' likely!

Then Lavinia spoke.

'Why,' she asked, 'do you want to join that boy's
gang?'

Figgy was taken aback.

'How d'you know about that?'

'Well, I have two ears, you know.'

'Bloomin' big ones!'

'Mummy says only people with a limited vocabulary swear.'

'Who's swearing? "Bloomin' " ain't swearing.'

'You *meant* it as a swear word, and that's what counts.'

'Blimey!'

Lavinia ignored the 'Blimey!'

'Why do you want to be friends with that Basher boy?'

Figgy did not answer. In the first place, it was none of her business; and, in the second . . . well, in the second, he did not think he could explain.

'He's not very nice, you know,' Lavinia said.

And then Figgy dimly realised that that was half the answer.

Basher wasn't very nice. He said and did things that were not at all nice. And being as nice as Mr and Mrs Figg expected a son of theirs to be was quite a strain. There were times when Figgy longed to be plain bad.

'He's a bully,' went on Lavinia. 'He's not really much good at anything himself, and he just wants little boys like you that he can boss around.'

Little!

Whatever sense Lavinia might be talking was blasted into atoms by that word again. Figgy's mind clawed and scrabbled to find something hurtful to

49

throw back at her. But all he could put his tongue to was Basher's taunt.

'None of your business, *Lav*!'

Lavinia did not answer back, nor did she show any sign of being in the least put out. She really didn't!

More than ever, Figgy hated her.

After washing up, Mrs Figg settled in a deckchair for a quiet read, and Lavinia lay on the grass beside her with a book as well. Mr Figg was dozing under the Sunday paper in the front room, and Peter had gone round to a mate's house to do some weight training. Figgy withdrew to the leafy branches of the apple tree with an armful of comics to keep him company. The lazy minutes dawdled by, and he was struggling to keep his heavy eyelids open when a squeal of terror from Lavinia almost brought him tumbling from his perch.

'Oh, I'm sorry, Auntie.' It was Lavinia speaking. 'I'm sorry but I just can't touch it.'

'It's only a picture, Lavinia,' said Mrs Figg.

'I know. It's silly, but I can't help it, I really can't.'

'What's up?' called Figgy, breaking cover.

'Never you mind,' said Mrs Figg. 'I'm going in to get the tea, so I'll want you in soon with those hands washed.'

Figgy could hear only snatches of conversation as Lavinia and Mrs Figg gathered up their things and went indoors. He wished the apple tree were not such a perfect hiding place, and itched to know what it was that Lavinia could not touch. It wasn't until he was rinsing his fingers at the kitchen sink that he heard Mrs Figg talking in her doctor's waiting room voice to Mr Figg.

'You know, she's that frightened of spiders she couldn't even pick up that library book of mine, the one with a spider on the cover.'

So, that was all, thought Figgy. At any rate, it was good to know she wasn't perfect. Frightened of spiders! Typical! Actually, Figgy couldn't touch real ones himself — but too frightened to pick up a picture! Really!

One reason for Figgy's keeping up the apple tree throughout the afternoon was to avoid being caught in any plans for entertaining Lavinia that evening. All through tea he kept quiet, hoping he would not be noticed. He almost overdid it.

'Are you all right?' his mother asked. 'You're not sickening for anything, I hope.'

'Love-sickening,' Peter murmured, just loudly enough for Figgy sitting next to him to hear.

'What's that, Peter?' asked Mrs Figg.

'Nothing.'

'Nothing's made your brother go the colour of that beetroot. Leave the child alone. If he's going down with something, I don't want him getting all steamed up.'

'I didn't say nothing!' retorted Peter.

'That'll do,' warned Mr Figg.

An awkward silence fell round the table. Lavinia was still stranger enough to make family quarrels an embarrassment. She, meanwhile, was politely cutting her slice of Dundee cake into dainty fingers as though unaware that a vulgar squabble was being smothered before it could flare up into a blazing row.

Peter sulked for the remainder of the meal and announced that he was going to his mate's again and then on to the youth club.

Mrs Figg asked Lavinia if there was anything she would like to do, and Figgy held his breath.

Yes, Lavinia said, there was. 'Songs of Praise' was coming from her church at home. They'd recorded it three weeks ago, and she would like to watch that if she might.

'Of course!' said Mrs Figg. 'You'll want to look out for all the people there you know. And they might have done a close-up of you, Lavinia. They always pick out some children, don't they? Did you notice any cameras on you? Fancy! Having someone in the house who's been on television!' Wild horses, Mrs Figg concluded, would not tear her from her television set that evening.

The thrilling prospect of watching a hymn-singing programme in which Lavinia might appear rather put Figgy from his mother's mind, and she was taken unawares when he quietly said he thought he would go out and find some friends to play with.

'But don't you want to see Lavinia on the telly? . . . Well, just you be back before it's dark. Holidays or no holidays, I'm not having you roaming the streets till all hours.'

At the corner of Wellington Street, Figgy found Gogsie already waiting for him.

'Where you been?'

His glasses reflected the setting sun like the death-ray eyes of an alien in a science-fiction film.

'Got here as soon as I could,' said Figgy, blinking.

'I've been here for ages,' said Gogsie, still annoyed by Figgy's remarks that morning about his prowess as a fighter. 'Well, come on or we'll keep Basher waiting too. And don't go telling no one where we're going.'

'I won't.'

'You'd better not.'

Gogsie led the way to the small river that ran round one side, the oldest side, of Kirkston. The days when barges used to carry goods to and from the town were gone, and many of the warehouses and factories were derelict, the haunt of tramps, schoolboys and ne'er-do-wells. Gogsie and Figgy crossed an iron footbridge to the further bank and arrived at an area known locally as the 'diggings'. These were a dismal expanse of allotment gardens where the older men of Kirkston raised vegetables for the family table. It was a place of half-hearted lettuces and weary runner-beans. The air held the sharp tang of lime and soot and pungent smoke from fires that seemed to be forever smouldering but never bursting into flame. Each narrow plot of land had a shed at one end for the tenant's forks and spades and trowels and packets of this and tins of that, and — most important — a stool or chair on which its owner could take his ease and drink a flask of tea and smoke his pipe in peace.

At that hour of a Sunday evening the 'diggings' were deserted, and the boys ignored the notice which warned members of the public that they were not welcome.

'Anyhow,' said Gogsie, 'my grandad's got an allotment.'

'Where?' asked Figgy.

'Right over there. Boring, I think. Mum says Grandad spends half his time snoozing in his hut. Him and Grandma are on holiday, so me dad's got the key so he can come and water things.'

Figgy followed Gogsie along narrow paths to where the 'diggings' were bounded by a ditch and straggling hedge and the survivors of a line of ancient trees. Stopping at a gap and motioning Figgy to be silent, Gogsie peered intently round before diving through the gap and dropping down into the ditch.

It was clear from the trampled grass, hog-weed and meadowsweet that this was a route in constant use by

54

someone, and Figgy guessed they must be near the hide-out. The boys crept along the ditch, startling a blackbird which flew away with its loud 'tchook-tchook-tchook' of alarm. And then Gogsie halted. On the bank above them towered the stump of a great oak. The storm which had finally brought it down had not been strong enough to uproot it from the earth in which it had grown for centuries, but had snapped the hollow, sapless trunk, leaving the jagged stump like the keep of an abandoned castle.

Gogsie seized one of its overhanging roots and, placing his toes in familiar footholds, clambered up, swung over the sides of the stump and disappeared. Figgy scrambled after him, and when he was able to look inside he found it wider than he could have imagined and much deeper. The rotten, crumbling wood had been hacked and scraped away and the ground dug into. And crouched inside were the Gang: Basher, Gogsie, Snotts and Scratcher.

'Well, come on then,' growled Basher. 'Don't hang about up there where everyone can see you.'

Awkwardly, Figgy got one leg over and found himself sitting uncomfortably astride the jagged stump. As he got the other leg up and prepared to slip down to the floor of the den, he found the seat of his jeans was snagged on one of the spikes.

'I'm stuck!' he hissed.

'Come on!' Basher hissed back impatiently.

Figgy loosened his grip, and with a sound of tearing he slithered to the bottom, tumbling headlong on the others. When the cursing boys had freed themselves from the knot of arms and legs, Figgy tried to find out what had happened to his jeans. Although he twisted round he could not see the damage, but he could feel the rip running from the back of his thigh up to the seat.

'My mum'll murder me!' he moaned. 'What's it look like?'

They roared with unkind laughter.

'I like the fancy pants,' jeered Basher. 'All them rocketships.'

'Yeah,' said Scratcher. 'What you might call eye-catching.'

'How am I going to get home?' Figgy wailed. 'I can't go through the streets in jeans like this.'

'Better take them off then!'

'Suppose you think that's funny?'

'Yeah! A real scream!'

As often is the way, someone else's misfortune can cheer you up no end; and Figgy's accident made the Gang forget their annoyance at being dropped on. And so they laughed and went on making jokes until Scratcher said, "Ere, I've got an old badge in my pocket. Perhaps we can hold you together with this. Turn round then.'

Scratcher unfastened the murderous looking point of a 'Mickey Mouse' badge and tried to pin the torn jeans back into position. Figgy was punctured six times before the job was done. Once was a pure accident.

All this had upset the ceremony for admitting a new member to the Gang. But there came a moment when all the jokes and laughs about Figgy's jeans were ended and the boys looked to Basher to begin the real business of the meeting.

'Well,' said Basher, trying to sound important, 'do you want to join the Gang, if we'll let you?'

'Oh yeah!' said Figgy, as he sniffed the scent of rotting wood, and looked up at the gnarled walls of the oak stump with its little hole just the height for pee-ing through. To have the right to be in this place made him forget the torn jeans and the pin-pricks.

'Well, first you've gotta do something.'

'Yeah?' said Figgy. He felt his throat tighten and his tongue seemed suddenly too big for his mouth. 'What?'

'It's gotta be something dangerous, something you'd be in trouble for if you got found out or caught.'

'Oh,' said Figgy. 'What?' he asked again.

Basher glanced at the other members of the Gang. You could tell from their excited, expectant faces they knew what he would say.

'Not *what*,' said Basher. '*Who.*'

'Who?' Figgy could not understand. 'What d'you mean?'

'I mean that cousin of yours... Lav-what's-'er-name.'

58

'Lavinia!'

'Yeah, *Lavinia*. You've gotta get her. She's got to be taught a lesson, that cousin of yours, if you're going to be a real member of this Gang.'

Basher did not explain why Lavinia was in need of lessons. Figgy knew, and he knew better than to say. He knew what would happen to anyone who was idiot enough to tell Basher that a girl had made a fool of him. Besides, Figgy had grievances of his own and burst into a recital of what he had suffered at Lavinia's hands over the past four-and-twenty hours: turned out of his room, bored with all the marvellous things she was supposed to be able to do, sick of her stuck-up manners, tired of being shown up by her. He went on and on, without once hinting at what had hurt him most of all — that she kept on rubbing in that he was little.

'Right,' said Basher, growing impatient. 'So what are you going to do?'

Figgy suddenly ran out of words.

'Well, I don't know. I haven't thought.'

Snotts said, 'Why not push her out a window?'

'What!' cried Figgy.

'Yeah, that's dangerous,' said Scratcher.

'That's stoopid,' said Basher. 'They'd lock him up for life.'

'So what's stupid about that?' muttered Gogsie.

Figgy shot him a cold, hard look. He was right off Gogsie.

'But he's got to do something dangerous,' said Snotts. 'That's the rules.'

'So what did you do?' Figgy asked him.

Basher answered. 'Phoned up Mr Ironside during the dinner hour, he did, and said he thought his school was rotten.'

'And did Ironside know that it was Snotts?'

'No,' said Basher. 'He sort of whispered it.'

'He calls that dangerous!' exploded Figgy. 'And he expects me to *murder* my cousin.'

'I didn't say *murder*,' Snotts protested. 'I said push her out of a window. That's all.'

'And that's not murder?'

'No, she might only break a leg or something.'

'Yeah,' agreed Figgy, 'like her *neck*!'

'Now then, you lot. You gotta use this,' said Basher, tapping his head in imitation of his father.

'I tell you what,' said Figgy, 'I'll phone Lavinia and tell her I think she's rotten — and I won't whisper.'

'And that's dangerous?' jeered Gogsie.

'Will be if she tells my mum.'

'No,' said Basher. 'Won't do. Your precious Lav's gotta be taught a lesson, and I mean a *lesson*. So think.'

The silence that settled on the boys was broken by a high-pitched pinging. It was the alarm on Snotts' new, birthday, digital watch.

'Gotta go,' he said. 'If I'm not back by seven o'clock, I won't be allowed to watch the film on telly.'

60

'But nothing's been decided yet,' said Basher.

'I want to see that film too,' said Scratcher. 'The one with the car driving over the edge of a bridge and exploding when it hits the water.'

Basher gave the meeting up.

'All right. Come back tomorrow at six o'clock. And you'd better come up with a good idea, Figgy, or you might have to do what Snotts said after all.'

There was a scramble to leave the hide-out, for it was possible for only one at a time to clamber up the steep sides of the hollow stump. Figgy was the last. As he sat on the top, preparing to jump down, he remembered the torn seat of his jeans and the badge that pinned it up. The thought of its rusty point and the memory of the wounds he had already suffered made him nervous of some accident. Suppose as he leapt or landed the pin unfastened and was driven deep into his seat like a hypodermic needle.

As he hesitated, the others called impatiently.

'He's scared!' said Gogsie.

'A little jump like that!' Snotts exclaimed. 'I'm not waiting here all night for him.'

The jump itself did not frighten Figgy. He jumped. To his relief there was no agony of steel piercing tender flesh, but the effort of the leap and the impact of the fall as he tumbled in the ditch were too much for the fraying denim, and as Figgy struggled to his feet he realised that red and yellow spaceships were zooming

61

through deep blue space again for all the world to see.

''Ere, wait!' he called after the others who were already loping off along the ditch towards the opening in the hedge. 'It's me jeans again!'

But they didn't wait.

It's difficult to run stooping along the uneven bottom of a ditch, trying with one hand to hold the seat of your trousers in place. Figgy caught up with the Gang as they paused at the gap, checking that the coast was clear.

''Ere,' Figgy panted. 'I've come undone.'

'Tough!' said Basher. 'Right, come on.'

And off they set to cross the allotments. They were about halfway along the zig-zag route that led them to the bank of the canal when a fierce cry of *'Oi!'* made them spin round. As if from nowhere a man had appeared not a dozen steps behind them. The cry had sounded fierce, and the man who had uttered it looked every bit as fierce as he had sounded. An old man, but a fierce and fit old man who was capable of pursuit and bloody execution. This old man wasn't like teachers and policemen who would reason with you. If this old man caught you, he would belt you one.

'Get out of it!' he roared, brandishing a fork in one hand and a gigantic carrot in the other.

Without pausing to offer a single word of cheek, not even to make him a rude gesture, the boys took to their heels, terrified of being impaled on that avenging fork

62

or of being clubbed insensible by the carrot.

Figgy threw modesty to the winds. Both arms working like little pistons, he raced after the others, his only thought to escape this guardian demon of the 'diggings' and reach the safety of the tow-path.

The old man's threats and curses followed them.

'Little devils! .... I'll know you again .... Just let me lay my hands on you! .... Trespassing! I'll *trespass* you!'

Outside the allotments, secure from capture, the Gang stopped and sprawled on the ground, their courage returning faster than their breath.

'Blimey! Where'd he come from!' gasped Snotts.

'Must have been behind his hut,' Basher panted. 'Silly old twit!'

'D'you think he saw us coming from the hide-out?' Gogsie asked.

'No,' said Basher. 'But we'll have to be careful. If he's going to be watching out for us, we won't be able to go through the middle of the allotments like that. We'll have to go the long way round the edge.'

'That's miles!' Snotts argued.

'Well, what do you suggest we do?' Basher growled. 'Dig a tunnel?'

'Do you think he'll really know us again?' asked Figgy.

'Probably know your pants,' said Gogsie. 'Perhaps you'd better wear some different ones next time we come. Got any with steam engines or motorbikes?'

'Very funny!'

'All mine are plain,' said Scratcher, rather sadly.

'Shut up about your pants!' snapped Basher. 'Just remember, you lot, go the long way round in future and watch out for old Grandad.'

5

Taking Out a Contract

The journey home through the streets of Kirkston seemed to have doubled, and never before on a Sunday evening could there have been so many people wandering the pavements. And Figgy was convinced that they were all looking at him as he sidled along with one hand held awkwardly behind him. He was convinced that everyone was pointing and talking about him when he had gone past; and if he heard a laugh or a giggle he was certain it was his torn jeans that were being laughed at.

Glad though Figgy was to push open the gate of Number 17, it was with dismay at the thought of explaining to Mrs Figg about the tear. Really, life seemed an endless round of problems!

When Figgy went into the kitchen, he could hear the sound of hymn-singing from the front room; so Mum and Lavinia must still be watching 'Songs of Praise'. Perhaps he could slip upstairs and change into his other jeans. At least he could put off the fuss that was bound to come. But Mrs Figg called out: 'Is that you, Michael? Come in quick. You're just in time to see Lavinia!'

There was nothing for it, but to do as he was told. He

crab-walked into the room and sat down on the floor as quickly as he could with his back against the settee.

'Look, there she is!' cried Mrs Figg. 'Look — *there*! Oh, she's gone . . . . It looked just like you, didn't it, Lavinia? There's lots of people there Lavinia knows, aren't there, dear? — Look, that lady there — the one with the pearls, not the one next to her in the straw hat — that used to be Lavinia's teacher. What did you say her name was, love? Miss Mawson? — No, Miss Maldon, that's right.'

Figgy stared blankly at people in their Sunday best. Who on earth, he wondered, wants to watch a lot of people singing hymns? And who, in his right mind, would want to watch Lavinia? Well, Mrs Figg did and

Lavinia herself; and they remained, their eyes glued to the screen, until the priest had given the blessing and the credits began to roll.

'Well,' said Mrs Figg, 'after the excitement, I expect we'd like a cup of tea.'

Mr Figg woke up and agreed he would.

'And you, Michael?' his mother asked.

'Yes,' he said.

'And what's that little word?'

'*Please*,' he added.

'Yes, and you can come along and help me carry in the cups — No, Lavinia, you stay where you are. It won't hurt his lordship here to stir his stumps.'

Figgy remembered the jeans. The last thing he wanted to do now was to stand up before an audience.

'Come on, Michael . . . . Why are you standing there like that? What have you done? Turn round. What are you holding your hand like that for?'

Mrs Figg snatched his hand away, and the space rockets blasted into view. Lady though she was, even Lavinia could not suppress a little giggle.

Figgy's explanations did not satisfy his mother. He had no business to be climbing trees. This would not have happened if he'd stayed at home and kept his cousin company. Where did he think money was coming from to buy new jeans? Well, there wouldn't be any. He'd have to make do with patched ones. And so on, and so on . . . . At last, he was sent upstairs to change.

When he came down again, the film had started. It was difficult to understand what was happening. It seemed that there was one man who wanted to get rid of a woman, and he 'took out a contract on the broad'. Figgy worked out that this was American for paying someone else to kidnap and murder a woman. Events proved him correct. The female star was lured to a beach hut, drugged, and the beach hut set on fire. That should have been the end of her, and Figgy would not have cared, but the male star, who played a private eye, broke in and carried the unconscious broad to safety. There were several more attempts to get her, and finally the baddy was caught in his own trap and perished in the exploding car described by Snotts.

Over the supper-snack the Figgs always had on Sunday nights, Mrs Figg chattered about plans for the next day. What would Lavinia like to do? Was there anywhere she'd like Michael to take her? Lavinia didn't think so, and, in any case, she didn't want Michael to have to stay with her. She was sure he would rather be out playing with his friends.

She was right — but it irritated Figgy the way she sounded so grown-up and talked about him as though he was, well, a little kid.

'Nonsense!' Mrs Figg declared. 'Michael would enjoy your company. Perhaps you can keep an eye on him and see he doesn't go tearing the seat out of every pair of trousers he possesses.'

Even Peter's coming in made a welcome interruption. After gobbling up the remaining sausage rolls and sandwiches, he announced he was going to have a bath and ran upstairs.

'And it's time you were off to bed as well, young Michael,' said Mrs Figg. 'Five minutes more and then up you go. You know what you're like if you don't get your sleep.'

When he got upstairs, Figgy could hear Peter splashing in the bath, probably playing with the plastic boats that were supposed to be his, Figgy's. He'd caught Peter at it once before and Peter had been furious. So he turned the handle sharply, hoping to surprise him. But the door was bolted. The splashing stopped.

'What do you want?' called Peter.

'Nothing.'

'Oh, it's you. Shove off!'

Figgy slouched into Peter's bedroom and dropped down moodily on the bed. Nothing was right. Lavinia, the torn trousers, the problem of doing something dangerous for the Gang, Peter and that note — Peter and that *note*! As he thought that thought, he realised that he was looking at Peter's clothes strewn across the floor where he had dropped them: trainers, socks, pants (red and blue stripes), T-shirt, jeans and *denim jacket*! From the splashing in the bathroom it was plain that

69

the Battle of the Atlantic was still raging. There was time to see if Peter had left the note in the pocket. He picked the jacket up, undid the zip and felt inside. Figgy's heart leapt when he found a sheet of folded paper. He pulled it out. The relief! Destroy this, and that was one of his problems solved. At least he would have Peter off his back. But before he tore it into little pieces, he unfolded the paper. And in that moment he was plunged back in despair. What his eyes rested on were not the lines and lines of insults he had written, but one sentence in heavy capitals.

DEAR DIM LITTLE BROTHER, KEEP YOUR THIEVING FINGERS OFF MY THINGS.

It wasn't fair!

He was still standing there with the sheet of paper in his hand when Peter entered.

'Now come along, Michael,' he said, grinning broadly, 'it's high time you were in bed. When you're all tucked up I'll tell you a story.'

Figgy didn't have much fight left in him. He screwed the paper up and threw it to the floor. Then silently he undressed and crawled into his sleeping-bag. Peter stood in front of the mirror on the wardrobe flexing his muscles and looking very pleased with what he saw.

It wasn't fair!

They were brothers, so why were they so different? Peter was big and had muscles, there was no denying it, and he was a lovely golden brown; while Figgy was

70

short and thin and weedy, and if he went sunbathing he just turned red and peeled.

Peter switched on his bedside lamp, making black the summer night framed in the window, and sat cross-legged on his bed to cut his toe nails.

'I've been wondering,' he said, 'what you might do tomorrow.'

Figgy did not answer.

'Well, don't you want to know?'

'No!'

'You do surprise me! Somebody as nosy as you! Now, thinking about tomorrow. You must admit today you've had it easy. A cup of tea this morning and accompanying the Loverly Lavinia to the park, that's all. To recompense me for keeping that unfortunate letter safe from prying eyes you will want to do more than that. So I thought, I know, Michael would like to clean my bicycle. Really get the chrome rims sparkling, oil the cogs and chain, polish up the bars: all that sort of thing. I'm going out for a run with me mates in the afternoon, so if you can get it done before dinner time that will be fine . . . . Night, night! Sleep tight!'

Peter slipped between the sheets and in a few moments he was sound asleep.

But Figgy lay awake, his mind going round and round the same old problems: Lavinia, the note, the Gang, Lavinia, the note, the Gang, Lavinia, Lavinia, Lavinia . . . . Everything started and ended with

71

Lavinia. If Lavinia hadn't come, he wouldn't have run away, he wouldn't have written that note, Peter wouldn't have found it, Basher wouldn't have been insulted, and he wouldn't have to get revenge on Lavinia for Basher's sake. Lavinia he had to put up with until she went away, and Peter and his blackmail he would have to put up with until he got the note back or until Peter got fed up with it. But something had to be done quickly if he was to get into the Gang. He had to have some plan for when the Gang met again next evening. Bother Lavinia! He wished someone would put a contract out on *her*. He'd make sure no one butted in to save her. No hero kicking in the doors of beach huts — *Huts*!

'. . . must have been behind his hut . . . .'
'. . . spends half his time snoozing in his hut . . . .'
'. . . on holiday . . . .'
'. . . Dad's got the key . . . .'
You couldn't set fire to it, of course. But . . . perhaps
 . . . !

Figgy and Peter both slept late next morning, and it was Lavinia washed, hair brushed, immaculately dressed who knocked and put her head into the room.

'Auntie says if you want any breakfast you must come down now . . . . It's a lovely day.'

The boys blinked at her grumpily, but did as they were told. Figgy crept downstairs in his pyjamas, Peter in his dressing gown.

'Honestly, I'm ashamed of you!' their mother scolded. 'What a spectacle!'

Figgy and Peter munched their cornflakes. Mrs Figg was already washing up the breakfast things while Lavinia did the drying. Mr Figg had left for work several hours before.

'Now what are you children going to do today?' asked Mrs Figg.

'Michael's cleaning my bike this morning,' Peter said.

'What? Is he joking, Michael?'

'No.'

'Well, I don't know what's come over you. I know you ripped your trousers yesterday, but I've got to admit I've never known you so thoughtful and so helpful . . . and what are you going to do, Lavinia?'

'Oh, I'll catch up on my violin practice, Auntie. And then I'm sure there's something I can do to help you.'

'Monday's one of my days for washing, but when I've loaded the machine perhaps you'd like to come down to the shops with me.'

When Figgy came downstairs again, after getting washed and dressed, he found Mrs Figg sorting out the clothes ready for putting into the washing machine, and talking to Lavinia who was sipping another mug of tea.

' . . . and if I didn't go all through their pockets

73

goodness knows what would go into the wash —
handkerchieves, sweets, money — pound coins I've
found in your uncle's! — conkers, pens. I can't begin
to tell you!' said Mrs Figg. 'I mean, just look at this!'
She held up a large marble fished from a pair of
Figgy's jeans. 'Imagine what would have happened
if that had gone spinning round in my machine!'

Figgy tried to slip out into the garden.

'And where are you going?' Mrs Figg demanded.

'The garden. I've got to clean Peter's bike.'

Mrs Figg, busy with the washing and Lavinia's
company, did not ask what Figgy meant by 'got to',
and he was safely out of the kitchen before she could
think about it.

Peter's bike stood in the shed at the bottom of the
garden. It was an expensive racer, a combined
birthday and Christmas present. His birthday was on
the 27th December and Peter always claimed that he
never really got a birthday present, just Christmas
presents left over from the 25th; but Figgy saw it
differently and complained that Peter always got
something special while he had to put up with little
things!

There was no doubt that it was a really splendid bike.
The frame was an electric blue and the twelve gears
and dropped handlebars promised scorching speed.
Peter took good care of it; there were no scratches or
spots of rust, but the dusty roads of summer had dulled

the gleam of the rims and the hubs were thick with dirt. It was going to be a long job.

With an oily rag Figgy set about his task. It was fiddling, difficult to get right round the spokes and especially to reach all parts of the rear axle. His fingers were soon grimed with dirt and grease.

From the house came the unfamiliar sounds of a violin. Twangs and scrapes — Lavinia tuning up. Scales, up and down, repeated when wrong notes squealed, and then her 'pieces' — nothing you could whistle. On and on. Lavinia wasn't one of those who did her twenty minutes just and then escaped.

Suddenly, Peter stood there in the doorway, blocking out the sunlight.

'Making a good job of it, are we?'

He examined Figgy's work critically.

'Not bad, not bad. I'll tell you what, Michael,' he said brightly, 'you make a really good job of that and I might let you do it for me regularly.' He laughed and turned to leave; stopped and looked back. 'Of course, if you don't make a really good job of it, you'll have to do it all again.'

Figgy burned with hatred. Bully! He knew the sort of job he'd like to make of Peter's bike. Serve him right if he fixed it. Mucked the brakes up — loosened the nuts that held the wheels in place! He wouldn't be so cocky if it fell to pieces under him. But that was just a spiteful daydream. The police had come to Figgy's school and

he knew how dangerous it was to do anything like that. The photographs they'd been shown of kids who'd come off their bikes were terrible.

When he had finished, Figgy skulked at the bottom of the garden until Mrs Figg called out: 'We're just going down the shops, Lavinia and me. Won't be long. Be good!'

Figgy went into the bathroom to try to wash his hands. There was dirt ground into the cracks of the skin and under his nails that nothing would get out. He left the basin with mucky smears and an oily tide-line.

'Did you hear Lavinia practising?' asked Mrs Figg as they sat down to dinner. 'She's got the touch all right. I can't imagine how you get all that music out of it by just scraping a few strings.'

'Michael was saying he wished he could learn,' said Peter.

'Really?' said Mrs Figg before Figgy could deny it. 'I didn't think he liked the violin. He always says it's like cats screaming,' she told Lavinia. 'Perhaps hearing you do it properly has changed his mind.'

'I don't mind showing him how to start,' Lavinia said. 'That's if he'd like to.'

'Now, dear, that is nice of you. Why don't you go off now, if you've had all the apple pie you want.'

Figgy could only trail after her, upstairs to his bedroom. The lesson was an agony to him and to everybody else in earshot.

'I don't think Michael's really got the feeling for the violin,' Lavinia said.

'I expect you're right,' sighed Mrs Figg. Relief at being spared the torment of Figgy's daily practice went a long way to make up for her disappointment.

And Figgy, meanwhile, loathing Lavinia more than ever, hoped and prayed his plans for her were workable.

He managed to escape in time and set off for the allotments. He went on his own. At the gate he paused, nervously. Few people seemed to be working there, but after yesterday you could not be too careful. Finding all the cover that he could, just like the people on the telly, he skirted the boundary of the plots until, at last, unchallenged he reached the gap, slipped into the safety of the ditch and made straight for the hide-out. He was not the last one there; Scratcher was yet to come. They crouched in the bottom of the stump waiting for him, while the woodlice scurried in and out of cracks and overhead a jet plane unzipped the sky.

At last, they heared the sounds of someone scrabbling up the tree and Scratcher's head hung over them.

'Come on!' Basher called. 'We've been waiting ages.'

Scratcher dropped down among them.

'Sorry. I had to look after my baby sister while me mum was round me gran's.'

'Well,' Basher said to Figgy. 'What are you going to do?'

'Did you all see the film last night?'

'Yeah.'

'No,' said Gogsie. 'Dad wanted to watch the other side. Was it good?'

'Yeah — but the thing is it gave me an idea.'

'What?' growled Basher, obviously puzzled.

'You know this man paid these other men to kidnap this woman . . . ?'

'His sister?'

'Yeah, that's right,' said Snotts. 'And they trapped her in this hut thing.'

'Well, I thought we could do the same thing to Lavinia.'

'What! Knock her out and set the hut on fire?' jeered Scratcher.

'No, 'course not! I mean we could just kidnap her for a bit and frighten her.'

''Ere,' Basher interrupted. 'You keep on saying *we*. *You're* the one who's supposed to be doing this.'

'But she knows *me*.'

'I expect she does.'

'No, look, I can't actually do the kidnapping. She knows me. What I've got to do is put out a contract on her.'

'What?'

'You know, like in the film. Get some other people to do it.'

'I don't understand,' said Gogsie.

'Look,' said Figgy. 'Your grandfather's got an allotment, ain't he?'

'Yeah.'

'And he's got one of these hut things?'

'Yeah, but . . . ?'

'And your dad's got the key while he's on holiday?'

'Yeah.'

'Can you get the key?'

'Dad leaves it hanging on our keyboard in the kitchen.'

Basher butted in. 'What are you trying to say?'

'Well, I was wondering if we couldn't catch Lavinia somehow and shut her up in Gogsie's grandad's hut.'

The idea was appealing.

For a minute no one spoke. Eyes were blank as the minds behind them raced, trying to work out what it really meant. Mouths gaped slightly with the effort.

Snotts spoke first.

'I don't see how it could work.'

'Why?' asked Figgy.

'Well, how could we get her over here?'

'I could bring her on a walk. Mum's on at me all the time to take her out for walks.'

'Sounds like a dog,' said Gogsie.

'Shut up!' Basher said.

'But she'd know us,' added Snotts.

'No,' said Figgy. 'You could wear masks, stockings over your heads, like bank robbers.'

'But if you're with her,' Basher said, 'we'd have to kidnap you.'

'I'll leave her.'

'Then she'll know you're in it.'

'I'll think of an excuse.'

'Like what?'

'Well... I'll say I need to go behind a hedge or something.'

'Still think it's a bit obvious,' said Snotts.

'Not if I'm the one who rescues her.'

'You beat us four!' Basher sneered.

'No, not then, later. A lot later. I'll say I've been looking all over for her and at last I found this hut. See?'

'Hmm,' grunted Basher doubtfully. 'But if she's locked in how will you get her out?'

'You'll leave the key in the door.'

''Ere, wait a minute,' said Gogsie in alarm. 'I've got to get that key back on the hook before my dad comes home.'

'That's all right,' Figgy explained. 'I'll rescue her before tea time. You can be hiding somewhere and when we've gone you can get the key back.'

'Suppose,' said Basher, 'she tells your mum and dad — and she *will* — and they come and find which hut it was, and they find out it's Gogsie's grandad's?'

'Yeah!' said Gogsie. 'What about that, then?'

Everyone looked at Figgy.

'Well?' demanded Gogsie.

'You'll have to blindfold her and tie her hands behind her back.'

'Blimey!' Scratcher said.

'If she can't see where you take her, and if I hurry her away as soon as I've rescued her, she probably wouldn't know which hut she's been in.'

'Yeah, that's right,' Snotts said. 'She'll probably be a bit historical by then. Crying and all that.'

'I still reckon we're the ones who are taking all the risks,' said Gogsie. 'And it's supposed to be *his* dare.'

'Gogsie's right,' said Basher. 'If this goes wrong, we're the ones who are going to be in trouble.'

'Yeah!' said Gogsie.

'Yeah!' said Scratcher.

'It's a good idea though,' said Snotts.

'Suppose,' said Basher, 'suppose you signed a note saying it was all your idea, and if anything went wrong we showed them this note?'

'Yeah!' said Gogsie, Snotts and Scratcher. 'That'd be all right.'

But Figgy was not keen. Most of his troubles were the result of writing things, and he didn't like the idea of another piece of paper ticking like a time-bomb.

'Well....'

'I'm not doing it if he don't,' said Gogsie. 'And it's *my* grandad's shed.'

Gogsie had him there.

'Oh, all right,' he said.

Nobody had paper or pencil with him, so the contract could not be drawn up then and signed. This meant another delay, which disappointed everyone because they were all enthusiastic now to get on with the getting of Lavinia. But, as Basher pointed out, this was too big a job and too dangerous to be rushed into.

'So we meet again tomorrow,' he concluded. 'Can everyone make it here first thing?'

The only one who wasn't sure was Figgy.

'It all depends,' he explained, 'on Lavinia. Mum might make me take her out somewhere; and then there's Peter.'

'What's Peter got to do with it?' demanded Gogsie.

'Oh... nothing. He can be a bit awkward sometimes.'

Figgy decided not to tell about the blackmail.

6
The Lady Vanishes

Figgy was quiet at the tea table. He had a lot to think about. So he started guiltily when his mother said, 'And you needn't think I don't know what's about to happen.'

Before he could stammer an excuse, Mrs Figg went on.

'Yes, Lavinia love, we've not forgotten it's your birthday on Wednesday, and you needn't think your mum and dad have either. They sent quite a parcel through the post before they went on holiday.'

Lavinia's birthday! That's all she was on about. Of course she didn't know anything about the kidnapping. How could she?

'That's right, love,' said Mr Figg. 'Your auntie and me was wondering if there was anything special you might like to do.'

'Thank you,' said Lavinia. 'But, really, I don't know.'

'Well, you think about it, pet,' said Mrs Figg. 'We want you to have a really lovely day. We did try to think of something to surprise you. But, then, surprises aren't what people always want.'

No, they aren't, thought Figgy grimly.

'We thought about a party for you,' said Mr Figg, 'but apart from us you haven't had much chance to make new friends.'

'Not that we won't have a proper birthday tea,' Mrs Figg put in.

Ooh, more trifle! Figgy raised a silent cheer. It didn't make up for all the trouble Lavinia had caused him, but at least two lots of celebration trifle were because of her.

Peter had been rushing through his meal, and now he left the table to run upstairs. Mr Figg looked at Mrs Figg who nodded back at him.

'Yes,' she said. 'Got them this afternoon. It's his own money so there's not much we can say. Mind you, they'll need washing every time he takes them off and we all know who'll be doing that.'

'They seem to be starting younger and younger these days,' grunted Mr Figg. 'Only seems like yesterday he was still playing with his toys.'

'He still does!' Figgy grumbled. 'Leastways, he does with mine. Every time he has a bath he messes with my boats. And if I touch anything of his, he . . . .'

'All right, all right,' said Mr Figg. 'That will do. I expect you'll be the same when you reach his age.'

'I won't have any younger brother's things to mess about with!'

'Don't be silly,' said Mrs Figg. 'That's not what your father means.'

The cups and plates were being cleared away when Peter came downstairs again, dressed in a brand-new pair of dazzling white trousers.

'Hmm!' sniffed Mr Figg with disapproval. 'I suppose you *can* sit down in those?'

'Really, Peter!' said Mrs Figg.

Show off! thought Figgy.

'I'm going out,' muttered Peter through jaws that worked at gum. 'Expect me when you see me.'

'Oh no!' said Mr Figg. 'Ten o'clock. Not a minute later. Mind, I mean that.'

'Oh, all right,' said Peter. 'I'm not a kid, you know!'

'*Is* there anyone?' Mr Figg asked when Peter had left the room.

'Don't think so,' said Mrs Figg. 'Just that silly crowd of girls that hang about the youth club.'

'Of course, he is very handsome,' said Lavinia.

Figgy nearly choked.

'Er... takes after his father,' Mr Figg joked nervously.

'Well, it's high time we got these dishes washed,' said Mrs Figg. 'Are you going to give me a hand, Lavinia?'

Figgy was still awake and reading his comics when Peter came home not long after ten o'clock.

'Right,' he said, after he had kicked his shoes off, 'you can give me a hand with these.'

'You wanted tight ones,' Figgy growled. 'Anyhow, I'm not your servant.'

'Wrong!' sang Peter, lying on his bed. 'You'll do as I say. Get hold of the legs and pull.'

Grumbling all the time, Figgy tugged at the legs of Peter's trousers and inched them off.

'Ah, that's better,' Peter sighed. 'Now hang them over the back of the chair, you little grub, and then we'll think about your plans for tomorrow.'

'Oh, Pete!' protested Figgy.

'Pete is it? Not — what was it? — "smelly toe-rag"?'

'Be a sport.'

87

'It's not in the nature of smelly toe-rags to be sports. Now, it seems to me that apart from that painful interlude with the violin, you have neglected the Loverly Lavinia something shameful today, so I suggest you offer to take her for another walk tomorrow. There must be heaps of places you've not shown her yet. Don't forget. I shall want to hear all about it.'

Figgy muttered.

'What was that ugly little word?' cried Peter. 'I don't know where you hear such language. Well, sweet dreams, little brother.'

In darkness and in silence, Figgy vowed a dreadful vow. It was a long one and contained a lot more ugly little words. Peter, musing happily on the success of the white trousers and what Lucy Butler had said to Claire Thomas loud enough for him to hear, was untroubled by the fact that Figgy was swearing to get even with him.

At the breakfast table, Peter played his usual trick.

'Oh, Michael was wondering last night if Lavinia would like to go for another walk sometime today.'

Lavinia looked at Peter, and then hard at her cornflakes when she said, 'That would be nice. Will you be coming this time?'

'Good idea!' said Mrs Figg.

'Yeah,' said Figgy. 'Smashing!'

'Well, no, 'fraid not,' Peter answered hurriedly. 'I'm sort of fixed up all day. Another time, perhaps.'

'I do think,' said Mrs Figg, 'it would be nice if you did do something to make Lavinia's stay a nice one. I must say Michael's being very good, and he's cleaned your bike for you — though for the life of me I can't think what for.'

'I can't today,' said Peter. 'I've told you, I'm fixed up already.'

'Well, you can get unfixed.'

'Oh, no,' said Lavinia. 'If Peter's busy, it really doesn't matter.' And she concentrated once more on her cornflakes.

Figgy was disappointed that Peter had got out of going on a walk, though he couldn't imagine why Lavinia wanted him to come.

'Well, when are you going?' Mrs Figg enquired.

'Would this afternoon be all right, Michael?' Lavinia asked him. 'I said I'd go to the shops again with Auntie this morning.'

'Yeah,' said Figgy. '*Yeah*,' he said more brightly, 'that ought to be all right.'

Figgy was first getting to the hide-out. While he waited for the others to arrive, he enjoyed just sitting by himself inside a tree. It was slightly damp, and the sun which shone in a cloudless sky drew smells rich and earthy from the ground. Alone in here you might be anything and anywhere: a fearful monster in its den, or an escaped prisoner of war waiting until the enemy guards had tramped past.

His thoughts were interrupted first by Scratcher, then by Snotts and Gogsie, and last of all by Basher.

'I've got it,' Basher said, and pulled a sheet of paper from his pocket, and a pencil. 'Sign here, Figgy.'

'What's it say?'

'Yeah,' said the others. 'What's it say?'

'You can read, can't you?' Basher growled.

'Yeah, but can you write?' Gogsie blurted out.

'Shut your face, four-eyes!' Basher told him.

Gogsie shut it.

'What's it say?' asked Snotts.

Figgy read, with difficulty for Basher's spelling and his handwriting were poor.

'I mikul Fig say it was orl my idear to kidnape lavnear and the overs onley done waht i told them to.'

'That ain't how you spell my name,' said Figgy.

'So what? Want to make something of it?'

'No, no.'

'Are you going to sign it then?'

'Yeah, yeah, all right.'

Figgy wrote his signature at the bottom, and Basher put the contract back into his pocket.

'I think he ought to have signed it in his blood,' said Gogsie.

'And are you going to get it?' Figgy asked.

90

'Take no notice of the little twit,' said Basher. 'Now we've got to decide when to do the job.'

'This afternoon,' said Figgy.

'This afternoon!' the others gasped.

'Yeah,' said Figgy. 'This afternoon. I've got to take her for a walk this afternoon, and tomorrow's her birthday so I shouldn't think we'd get much chance then.'

'Well,' said Basher, 'is everybody free this afternoon?'

It seemed that everybody was, though Gogsie made a bit of a fuss, saying he *expected* he was, until Basher asked him sharply if he was or if he wasn't.

'Well, yes, I suppose,' he admitted.

'Then why couldn't you say straight off? Can you get the key O.K. — *yes* or *no*?'

'Yes — but I've got to have it back for half-past five, before my dad comes home.'

'Now, what else shall we need?' said Basher.

'Masks,' said Snotts. 'What'll we do for masks?'

'My sister's got loads of old tights,' said Scratcher. 'She never throws them away. I can pinch a couple.'

'Right,' said Basher. 'We can cut the legs off those and pull them over our heads.'

'Ugh!' said Snotts.

'What's the matter with you?' asked Scratcher.

'I don't want your old sister's tights over my head!'

'There's nothing wrong with my sister,' Scratcher

91

said. 'She baths every day. That's more than you do.'

'He don't even bath every week,' said Gogsie.

'Yes, I do — my mum makes me.'

'Well,' said Gogsie, sniffing, 'no one would think so.'

'What d'you mean?' demanded Snotts.

'Shut up!' Basher said. 'Right, Scratcher, you bring four legs with you.'

'I ain't gonna wear one,' muttered Snotts, but everyone ignored him.

'Right, what else then?' said Basher.

It was, at length, decided that they would need a scarf to blindfold Lavinia and some cord to tie her hands behind her back so that she could not take off the blindfold. Basher was to bring the scarf and Snotts agreed to find some cord. They were on the point of working out the details of just how and where to do the kidnapping when Figgy said, 'She'll shout. Someone might hear her — that old grandad.'

'She'll have to be gagged,' said Basher. 'What'll we use?'

'Sticking plaster's best,' said Snotts. 'You just stick it across her mouth.'

'Who's got sticking plaster?' Basher asked.

'We've got some Band-Aids in our bathroom cabinet,' said Figgy, 'but they wouldn't cover Lavinia's mouth. She's got a big one.'

They agreed to bring another scarf for gagging.

The plan was this. The others were to hide in the

ditch near the gap until Figgy brought Lavinia there. Then he'd say he thought he'd dropped his penknife near the allotment gates and run off, telling Lavinia to wait there for him. When he was out of sight, they would get her, tie, gag and blindfold her and take her to Gogsie's grandad's hut. Then they'd all go back to the hide-out until it was time for Figgy's 'rescue'.

'I hope there are plenty of spiders in your grandad's hut,' said Figgy.

'Why?' said Gogsie.

'Lavinia's scared stiff of them — she can't even bear to touch a picture of one.'

'Never mind about spiders,' Basher said. 'Just you remember to leave the scarves in the hut so's I can take them home.'

There was no difficulty in leading Lavinia that afternoon in the direction of the allotments; but Figgy grew less and less happy the nearer they came to them. When the Gang had separated that morning, the excitement had run high and they had found themselves talking in American accents as they settled the final details of the plan. Even Gogsie had said, 'O.K. you guys, see you all at a quarter after two.'

At the gates of the allotments, Lavinia said, 'It's got "Private" up there. I think we oughtn't to go in.'

'Oh, that's all right,' said Figgy. 'They don't really mind, not most of them . . . well, that's half the fun.'

'What is?'

'Seeing if you can get across without being seen. Like Red Indians — you know. Come on. Follow me.'

Figgy slipped through the gate and, bending double, began to make his way round the edge of the allotments to the hide-out. Behind him Lavinia followed, one eye on the look-out for the natives and one fixed suspiciously on Figgy.

At last they approached the gap and Figgy glimpsed Scratcher's head peeping over the top before it disappeared, someone having dragged him out of sight. More than ever Figgy wished he had never started this. And even now it was not too late to stop. He could just turn round and take Lavinia back, ahd she'd be none the wiser. But the Gang would. He'd never be allowed to join, and now he knew their secret hide-out what terrible revenge they'd take on him!

And so, trying to sound innocent, Figgy said: 'Oh, I've lost my penknife. I think I must have dropped it at the gates. I'll go and look for it. I won't be long.'

'I'll come with you,' Lavinia said.

'No, no,' said Figgy. 'You stay here.'

'Two pairs of eyes are better than one when you're looking for something.'

'No,' said Figgy, 'you've gotta stay here . . . there's more things I want to show you, and . . . and you'll get tired going all the way back there and then here again. Look, you sit down and have a little rest.'

He ran, hoping to have stopped all arguments. When he glanced back, he was relieved to see that Lavinia had sat down with her back most conveniently to the ditch. Figgy hurried on until a turn in the path took him out of sight, and then he stopped, panting, not so much from the running as from his nervousness. After a minute, he looked cautiously round the shelter of a hut to see if anything were happening. He was in time to witness all.

From the ditch, four hooded figures were emerging. (Snotts must have given in about Scratcher's sister's tights.) At least, three emerged, the fourth slipped back, and the noise must have startled Lavinia who turned. Her attackers hesitated for a moment, then they fell on her. According to the plan, Snotts and Scratcher were to seize her arms, while Basher blindfolded her and Gogsie fixed the gag; then Lavinia's hands would be tied behind her and she would be bundled off to Gogsie's grandad's hut. And that was all there was to it — or should have been.

Lavinia's performance with the football should have warned the boys that she might not prove to be a damsel in distress. But, if they had not suspected it before, they knew it now. Lavinia laid about her with fists and feet and knees with a ferocity which made Figgy glad that he was out of it. He saw Snotts double up and fall writhing to the ground and Scratcher stagger back clutching at his nose. For a moment,

Figgy thought that Lavinia was going to overcome all four single-handed, but in the end the weight of numbers told and she was blindfolded, gagged and bound. Then they hustled her away, and Figgy ran to catch them up. Puffing and blowing they bundled her into the hut and Gogsie turned the key.

'Blimey!' gasped Scratcher when Figgy joined them. 'She's made my nose bleed.' He looked revolting. The stocking mask flattened his features and was stained with blood and spit and sweat.

'Shut up!' hissed Basher. 'She's got ears, ain't she? Come on. Back to the hide-out before anyone starts talking.'

Inside the hut, Lavinia kicked the door, kicked the walls, kicked everything. They heard the clatter of spades and forks and the crash of boxes. Gogsie looked appalled.

'Blimey! She'll smash everything!'

'Well, we can't let her out now,' said Basher. 'It probably sounds worse than it really is. Come on — back to the hide-out.'

Safe inside the tree stump, the boys examined their wounds and talked about the kidnapping.

'I said from the beginning,' Gogsie whined, 'I said that we was doing all the dirty work — and it's supposed to be *his* dare.'

'Yeah,' said Snotts, who still nursed himself, 'she

don't fight fair, she don't!'

'If anything's bust in that shed, I'm telling,' Gogsie threatened.

'I notice Figgy didn't come back till she was locked up safe,' said Snotts.

'Well, that was the plan, wasn't it?' said Figgy. 'You lot were in disguise.'

'You could have put a mask on too,' said Snotts.

'Yeah,' Scratcher said, 'you could've done.'

'No, I couldn't,' Figgy said. 'She knows me too well. She knows what I'm wearing and all that. And don't forget, I've got to rescue her. And I bet there'll be a lot of trouble because I wasn't there when you lot got her.'

'Hope there is,' said Gogsie, spitefully.

The slow minutes wore on in bad-tempered talk like this until at last half-past three arrived, the time appointed for Lavinia's rescue. The others stayed inside the hide-out in case she found her way back to the place where the kidnapping had occurred. The Gang would follow fifteen minutes later to collect the scarves and get the key for Gogsie.

On his own, then, Figgy set off for the shed, rehearsing what he'd say when he released Lavinia. As he drew near, he heard no sounds of kicking. She must have grown tired of that. In fact, there was total silence. Figgy was approaching the hut from the back, so that it wasn't until he turned the corner that he saw the door was open wide and Lavinia... Lavinia was gone!

7

The Broad Does a Deal

Figgy stumbled inside and stared wildly round at tools strewn over the floor. And still Lavinia was gone. How had she escaped? What was she doing now? — *Telling,* of course! He'd done it this time! Suddenly, he just wanted to run away and hide. He turned and raced back to the tree stump.

The others were surprised to see him.

'What d'you want?' asked Basher.

'She's gone!' squealed Figgy. 'She's not there.'

'What d'you mean "not there"?'

'What I said. Not there. She's gone!'

'Well, where is she?' Gogsie stammered.

'How do I know?' Figgy snapped.

'Gone to the police, I bet,' said Snotts.

'Oh, no!'

There was silence, and each boy strained his ears for the wail of sirens and the howls of tracker dogs.

'It's all his fault!' cried Gogsie. 'It says so on that paper.'

'Yeah,' said Basher, feeling for the contract in his pocket.

'You're the ring-leader. You're the one to blame.'

All at once, anger made Figgy blaze.

'Perhaps I am. But you're all in it too. And if they get
me I'll tell them who helped me. I'll tell them who got
the key. I'll tell them . . . .'

'Oh, blimey!' Gogsie exclaimed. 'I gotta get that
key. Come with me.'

'Not likely!' Scratcher said.

It was Gogsie's turn to threaten.

'All right, if I can't get that key back, I'll tell your
sister how you pinched her tights. And I'll tell on the
rest of you. I didn't want to do this in the first place.'

There was a lot more arguing until Snotts said at
last, 'We're wasting time. I vote we all go and get
Gogsie's key and the other things.'

'What other things?' said Scratcher.

'Basher's scarves and my string.'

'Blimey! I'd forgotten those,' said Basher. 'We don't want any clues left.'

Nervously, the Gang crept back to the shed. When Gogsie saw the state that it was in, he gasped.

''Ere, we've got to get this sorted out. My dad'll murder me.'

'He's right,' said Snotts. 'If anyone comes looking we want it to look absolutely normal.'

'Yeah, we don't want any clues,' said Basher. 'Where's my scarves, Figgy?'

'I don't know.'

'But they're not here.'

'*The key*!' shrieked Gogsie. 'It's gone! It's not in the door!'

'It must be.'

'It ain't! Look for yourself!'

'Perhaps it's on the floor.'

The boys searched, but there was no trace of the key, nor of Basher's scarves, nor of Snotts' bit of string.

'What am I going to do?' wailed Gogsie.

'Oh, shut up!' said Basher. 'This is all your fault, Figgy. If you'd rescued her like we'd planned, none of this wouldn't have happened.'

Figgy decided it wasn't worth protesting. Instead, he said, 'What are we going to do?'

'Well,' said Basher, 'for a start, we're clearing out

of here.'

'Figgy had better find out what's happened to Lavinia,' said Snotts. 'I expect the police are round his place. Perhaps we could all meet and . . . .'

'Oh, no!' said Basher. 'We don't want to be seen together. I dare say we'll hear what's happened soon enough.'

Gogsie was still whimpering, 'What about my key?'

'Tough!' said all the others. And the Gang split up to steal off to their homes.

Many, many times Figgy had not looked forward to going home, but never less than he did now. When a police car overtook him, he half expected detectives to spill out and seize him. Kidnapping was a serious offence. Thank goodness they hadn't sent a ransom note!

When he reached Stanley Road, he first peered round the corner, but no cars stood outside Number 17 and no constable was on duty at the gate. Everything was very quiet. Perhaps they were all down at the police station. Figgy slipped into the kitchen to find Lavinia sitting at the table with an open book and nibbling biscuits.

'Hello,' she smiled. 'Did you find your penknife?'

She was an amazing girl.

With a clean T-shirt and dungarees, her face washed and her hair brushed, she sat there as though she had not, only an hour before, been the victim of a violent kidnapping.

'Penknife?' Figgy mumbled, unable to keep up.

'Yes. You lost your penknife and went to look for it. You wouldn't let me come. Remember?'

'Yes.'

'Yes, you found your penknife, or yes, you remember?'

'No. I mean, it was in my pocket after all.'

'That's good . . . . Want a biscuit?'

'Er, no thanks.'

'I've found some things this afternoon.'

'Oh,' said Figgy, with rising panic.

'Can you guess what they are?'

'No . . . no . . . .'

'Well, here's one of them,' said Lavinia, taking the shed key from her pocket and putting it on the table.

'It's a key,' said Figgy.

'You know Auntie's wrong,' replied Lavinia. 'You're really quite a bright boy. And what do you think these are?' From her lap she took Basher's scarves and Snotts' bit of string.

'Oh, blimey!' Figgy said.

'Really, Michael!' said Lavinia. 'You and your friends! I suppose there is a ransom note somewhere.'

'Oh, no, no!' said Figgy. 'Nothing like that. We were going to let you out after an hour. Honest!'

'I'm sorry I couldn't stay that long. It must have

spoilt your game.'

'Who let you out?' asked Figgy.

Lavinia laughed.

'I let myself out, of course. For a start, whoever tied my hands had better join the Scouts and learn something about knots. Then, the next time you decide to lock someone in a shed, don't leave the key in the door. All I had to do was poke it out with a screw-driver and then reach under the gap at the bottom. Honestly, as soon as you peeped round that shed when you were supposed to be looking for a penknife I guessed something like this was up. Another second and Basher and his crowd wouldn't have had a chance.'

'How d'you know it was them?'

'Well, they weren't exactly silent.'

'Have you told Mum yet?'

''Course not!'

'Aren't you going to?'

'Of course I'm not!'

Figgy could scarcely believe his own good luck. He felt he almost liked Lavinia.

'Thanks a lot!' he said. 'Look, d'you think I could take that key back to Gogsie? He'll get into awful trouble if he can't get that shed locked before his dad comes home. And Basher wants those scarves. Don't think it really matters about the string.'

Lavinia guarded the objects with her hands.

'First, don't thank me too soon. And second, it

depends. I've got conditions.'

Figgy did not understand, at first. His Aunt Doris had a 'condition' — it was her bad feet. And his grandad had a 'condition' — that was the way he coughed every time he lit a cigarette. Figgy stared blankly at Lavinia.

'What I mean,' she explained to him, 'is that I'll let you have the key back and the scarves if Basher and his friends apologise to me.'

'But Basher never says sorry to anyone. And, besides, there's the contract.'

'What do you mean, "contract"?' asked Lavinia.

'Well, I signed a contract saying it was all my idea.'

'Was it?'

'Yes in a way. You see I had to do something dangerous to join the Gang. And all Basher'll do if anyone tries to blame him is to show that contract.'

Lavinia laughed.

'You don't really think anyone would take the slightest notice of that contract? Honestly, you boys!'

'But they might,' persisted Figgy.

'Very well,' Lavinia said. 'In that case, Basher and his mates will have to hand over the contract as well as apologising. And you can tell them,' she went on, silencing Figgy's objections, 'that if they don't I *will* tell on them. And just think what grown-ups will make of four boys setting on one helpless little girl.'

Figgy's mouth dropped open. Lavinia — a helpless

little girl!

'Well, those are my conditions: an apology and your contract back. You'd better get a move on, Michael, if that boy is to get his key back in time. Tell them to meet me at the scene of the crime by' — Lavinia glanced at her watch — 'by five o'clock. If they're not there, I shall go straight to Uncle and Auntie and complain.'

Somehow Figgy managed to persuade or frighten everyone into going back with him to the allotments, though Snotts and Basher still accused him of having told on them.

'I tell you, I didn't!' insisted Figgy. 'She recognised you.'

'Liar!' Basher growled.

'Oh, shut up!' said Gogsie. 'I don't care how she knows or what she wants, so long as I can get that key back.'

'Here she comes,' said Figgy.

The Gang fell silent and stared at Lavinia as she strode towards them along the narrow paths.

'Ah,' she said, 'the Mafia of Kirkston!'

'What she mean?' Snotts muttered.

'Shut up!' said Basher.

'Well?' Lavinia continued. 'Michael's told you what I want if I'm to hand these items over?'

'How d'you know we won't just take them?' Basher said.

'Oh, yeah!' Lavinia mimicked him. 'You and whose army?'

'Shut up, Basher!' Gogsie said. 'I gotta get that key back — *quick*!'

'Well,' Lavinia repeated. 'I'm waiting. What shall we begin with? — The contract, I think.' She held her hand out.

Basher glared at Figgy, then pulled the grubby scrap of paper from his pocket and thrust it into Lavinia's hand.

'Goodness gracious!' said Lavinia. 'I don't think a document as mis-spelled as this could be legally binding or used in evidence against anyone. It could mean almost anything. Someone's not been learning his spellings, has he!'

Basher actually ground his teeth. Figgy had read in stories of people grinding their teeth, but he had never heard it in real life. It was not nice. He glanced nervously at Basher's face. It was no nicer.

'And now,' Lavinia was saying, 'the apologies. Who shall be first? I think it should be you, Michael — after all, it was your idea and I am your cousin.'

'Sorry, Lavinia,' Figgy mumbled.

'And now the rest of you.'

One by one, Gogsie, Snotts and Scratcher said their 'sorries'. Only Basher hesitated. Lavinia looked him in the eye unblinking. The others held their breath.

'Sorry.'

'Thank you,' said Lavinia. 'Your apologies are accepted. And these belong to you.'

Gogsie took his key and raced to lock the door. Basher snatched his scarves.

'If we don't hurry now,' Lavinia said to Figgy, 'we shall be late for tea.' She turned and walked away.

'I'll get her!' Basher swore. 'And you, Figg!'

'It weren't my fault,' protested Figgy. 'What could I do?'

'So why'd she want that contract back if you hadn't been blabbing to her?'

Scratcher and Snotts turned on him too.

'Hadn't you better run after your big girlfriend?' Basher sneered. 'I mean she'll look after you if any rough kids pick on yer!'

'I can look after myself,' said Figgy.

'Oh, yeah!'

'Yeah!'

Pushing with chests and shoulders, the preliminaries of an all-out fight, began.

'Go on — 'it me then!' Basher dared him.

'He's chicken!' jeered the others. 'Cluck, cluck, cluck!'

'Go on — 'it me!' Basher said again.

Any moment now and fists and feet would fly, and Basher would wade into Figgy. Even with Figgy in a temper, there would be no contest.

It was a familiar bellow that startled them and saved

Figgy from a certain beating.

'I know you! ... Warned you off the other day! ... Tan your backsides raw when I gets 'old of you!'

Armed with a long dutch hoe, the old man charged at them and, taken by surprise again, Figgy and the Gang broke ranks and scattered.

8
Show Down

At the teatable, Mrs Figg seemed unaware that Figgy was in anything worse than his habitual glum mood. When she asked if they had had a pleasant afternoon, Lavinia told her they had been out for a walk and met some of Figgy's friends. Figgy had to admit it — Lavinia was a sport.

'Now,' said Mrs Figg, 'this birthday. Your uncle and me have had an idea. Suppose you children went to the fair that's come to town tomorrow evening? Now you don't want old fogies like us trailing round with you, so Peter will go and keep an eye on you.'

'Sorry,' said Peter, 'but I'm . . . .'

'But you're *nothing*,' said Mr Figg. 'It's Lavinia's birthday and it's her last day with us, and you're going to make a little effort to make it a happy day.'

'As well as your present,' went on Mrs Figg, 'we'll give you fifteen pounds to spend, so you should have enough for quite a few goes on all the rides and things. And when you get back there'll be a special birthday supper.'

'Trifle?' Figgy asked.

'I shouldn't be surprised. But I thought you'd gone off trifle, turning down second helpings the way you did.'

A trip to the fair with fifteen pounds to spend and trifle! True there'd be Peter mumping round and Lavinia, but, at least Figgy supposed, a girl like her wouldn't be frightened of going on the really exciting rides.

'I take it,' Mrs Figg said to the boys when Lavinia had left the room, 'that you have each got her a little something for her birthday?'

Their faces answered her.

'Well, of all the meanness! Just see that you go out first thing tomorrow and buy a present each. Goodness knows, you get enough pocket money!'

Now, if Figgy had a fault, it was that he disliked spending money, especially on other people. He much preferred counting money, building shining pillars of fifty-pence pieces, and, even better, slipping crisp new notes into the real leather wallet he had had for Christmas. The thought of having to part with hard cash for Lavinia gave him much the same sinking feeling as a visit to the dentist. And, in any case, what could you buy for girls?

The birthday dawned. Cards cascaded through the letter-box; parcels sent in advance were brought out from their hiding-places; and over breakfast Mrs Figg led the singing of 'Happy Birthday, Dear Lavinia', after which Figgy escaped on his mission to buy Lavinia a birthday present.

To his dismay, just down the road, lurking behind a pillar box, was Basher.

''Ere, Figgy!' he called to him.

Figgy hesitated. He could not forget that at their last meeting Basher had threatened to get him as well as get Lavinia.

'Figgy!' Basher called again. 'I wanna talk to yer.'

'Well?' said Figgy.

'I been thinking, see,' said Basher. 'I don't think I've been really fair with your Lavinia. I mean, she didn't tell on us, and she could have, couldn't she?'

'Yeah.'

'Well, we was pretty rotten to her, and I'd like . . . well, what I mean is . . . I've got a little present for her. I remembered you saying it was her birthday, see?'

He held out a small parcel wrapped untidily in brown paper and secured with sellotape.

'Give it to her, will you. Don't say it's from me. She'd want to say thank you, you know, and I don't want any of that.'

'What is it?' Figgy asked.

'Oh, it's nothing much,' said Basher. 'Couldn't afford much. It's just to show her how I feel. You will give it to her, won't you?'

'All right,' said Figgy.

'Cheers, mate,' said Basher, handing him the package. 'See you around.'

Basher was gone and Figgy was bewildered. He had

never known Basher to be sorry for anything, never admit that he was in the wrong. Yet the warmth of Basher's smile seemed genuine enough, and here in his hand was Basher's gift; there was no doubting that. Figgy felt a twinge of conscience. After all, Basher had got Lavinia a present and he wasn't even her cousin. But, at the same time, it occurred to Figgy that here was a present that would not cost a penny. There was no name on it, and Basher had made a point of saying he did not want Lavinia to know who it was from. Well, Lavinia would want to thank somebody, so it might as well be him.

Figgy wondered what Basher could have bought Lavinia. The parcel was very light. He shook it, but nothing rattled. Figgy shrugged his shoulders. What did it matter anyway? After all, it was only something to shut Mum up. Anything for a quiet life, as Mr Figg would often say.

To make it seem that he had been as far as the shops, Figgy strolled about the street for half an hour before returning to make the presentation.

'Well, here's another little surprise, unless I'm very much mistaken,' said Mrs Figg. 'Oh, what a scruffy parcel, Michael! Still, I suppose it's the thought that counts.'

'Happy Birthday,' Figgy said.

Lavinia smiled her widest smile.

'Oh, thank you! What is it, Michael?'

113

'Nothing much.' Figgy remembered Basher's words. 'It's just to show you how I feel... about yesterday, you know.'

'Yesterday?' said Mrs Figg suspiciously. 'What about yesterday?'

'It's nothing, Auntie,' said Lavinia. 'Just our little secret.'

She smiled again at Figgy and began to tear the sellotape. Mrs Figg and Figgy watched her undo the paper wrapping and reveal a cardboard box several inches square.

'This *is* exciting,' said Lavinia, as she began to ease the lid off.

A moment later, it was obvious that her excitement surpassed anything that could have been expected. Lavinia's screams rang in the ears and froze the muscles. Mrs Figg and Figgy both looked on in amazement before Mrs Figg could cry out 'Lavinia, whatever is it?'

Even as she screamed, Lavinia still held the box, her eyes fixed in terror on what she saw inside. Then Mrs Figg stepped forward, took the box from her niece's hand, and gave a little shriek herself when she saw what it contained.

It certainly was a big one!

Later, Figgy wondered where Basher could have found it. As it crouched in the box, it looked almost as big as the spiders in Tarzan films, the sort that crawl up

Jane's arm when she's sleeping in a tree. No doubt, this spider was just as frightened as Lavinia, and, if spiders screamed, its efforts would have equalled hers. Instead, it made a desperate bid for freedom by scrambling onto the hand that held the box. This was too much for Mrs Figg who, with another shriek, shook it to the floor. On seeing the creature at liberty and scuttling for the safety of the shadows beneath the sideboard, Lavinia's screams redoubled and did not stop until Mrs Figg dragged her out into the garden. And there she stayed, until Peter came back, tracked the spider down and flattened it with a folded copy of the *TV Times*, remarking as he did so that he could see more justice in flattening Figgy.

'What a wicked, wicked thing to do!' cried Mrs Figg, before seizing Figgy and hauling down his pants to administer a spanking which made her own hand tingle.

'But I didn't know it was a spider!' Figgy sobbed.

'Don't tell lies!' said Mrs Figg. 'You gave it to Lavinia.'

'No, I never. It was Basher.'

Little by little, Figgy told his story.

'Well,' concluded Mrs Figg, 'you still got what you deserve. And we'll make sure Master Basher gets what-for. I'll phone his mother, and, if I know Mrs MacIntosh, she'll give him something to remember.'

When Lavinia reappeared, she smiled sheepishly.

'Auntie, I'm so sorry. I know it's silly, but I just can't bear them, and I wasn't expecting it, and . . . .'

'Don't give it another thought, pet. At least, it seems Michael didn't give you a fright on purpose. Just a case of being a tight-fisted Scrooge, and a bit of a fool into the bargain. Still, let's concentrate on making the rest of your birthday a happy one. You've got the fair to look forward to — not that *some* people I could name deserve fairs, other people's birthdays or not other people's birthdays.'

Figgy was planning a quiet afternoon, up the apple tree with comics, well out of everybody's way where he could not possibly get into any trouble or be blamed for anything. He was on the point of sneaking down the stairs with a great armful of *Beanoes*, when he found Peter at the bottom blocking his escape.

'Well, little brother, tomorrow the Loverly Lavinia leaves us.'

'So what?'

'So, out of kindness, I am telling you that I have placed the note where Mum will find it before the day is out.'

'You toe-rag!'

'I will overlook that offensive remark, and I will even give you a clue . . . .'

'What?'

' . . . providing you give my bike another thorough spit and polish. I'll come to the shed in — shall we say an hour? — and, if the machine is spotless, you shall have a sporting chance.'

With the memory of the morning's walloping still painfully in mind, Figgy obeyed without a murmur; but in his heart, he vowed that when Lavinia was gone he would have revenge. And all the time that he was oiling, polishing and dusting Peter's bike he thought of ways to get his own back.

An hour later, Peter came as promised to inspect his work.

'Not bad, not bad at all,' he said. 'Credit where credit's due, you've made a real good job of that. I couldn't do much better, and that's a fact.'

'You could try,' said Figgy. 'Well, then, what's this clue?'

Peter sighed.

'Really, it's just a bit of advice. Don't let your troubles get you down — everything will come out in the wash.' He laughed as he strolled away. 'Thanks for all your help this week.'

'But you said you'd give me a clue!' Figgy shouted after him. 'You rotten toe-rag!'

It was typical of Peter. Rotten to the last. But where could he have put that note? Figgy searched everywhere: behind the candlestick where the family stuffed the bills and letters; in the kitchen cupboards; in the bathroom cabinet. And all the time, Figgy waited for the explosion when Mrs Figg should come across it.

And Lavinia? Birthday or no birthday, she was an angel to the end and had the day's washing in the machine and swirling round while Mrs Figg was still hoovering upstairs.

'A real mother's help!' Mrs Figg declared. 'You can come again, any time you like.'

Dusk was falling when Peter, Figgy and Lavinia set off for the fair. Half the magic of a fair, said Mrs Figg, was all the coloured lights at night-time, and with Peter there to watch them they could not get into any trouble. And as they reached the park, the roundabouts, the helter-skelter, the side-shows and the stalls were twinkling blue and red and green and yellow; and, over all, the great Ferris wheel revolved against the darkening sky.

Figgy and Peter were, of course, not speaking, and Peter's answers to Lavinia were of the briefest; nevertheless, she seemed very happy walking at his side and asking his advice about what amusements they should try.

Figgy was right: no matter what Lavinia's feelings were for spiders, she was game for any ride. And so an hour passed by in whizzing round on chair-o-planes, the ghost train and the dodgem cars, and eating candy-floss and popcorn.

But Peter grew more bored and sullen, sighing and looking at his watch every other minute; and, when at last a crowd of his mates and girls came by, he thrust what was left of Lavinia's fair money into her hand and said: 'I'll meet you here in half-an-hour, all right?'

Lavinia could not conceal her disappointment, but all Figgy said was: 'Good riddance!'

'What shall we go on then?' he asked Lavinia. 'We haven't tried the moon-rockets yet.'

'If you like,' Lavinia said, gazing after Peter who was chatting to a girl with bright green hair.

The moon-rockets spun you round, turned you upside down, hurtled towards the ground, then soared up into the night. You needed a strong stomach if you were not to lose your dinner. Figgy and Lavinia staggered, laughing, from the contraption. For a few minutes, Peter had been whirled out of Lavinia's mind.

'That was smashing!' Figgy said. 'I wouldn't mind another go on that. Have we got enough money left?'

'Just about,' Lavinia said. 'But we haven't been on the big wheel. It must be lovely right up there.'

'Oh, all right,' said Figgy. Well, it was Lavinia's birthday treat.

They made their way along the crowded lanes towards the great wheel. Figgy's eyes were lifted up, his mind so full of imagining what it would be like floating up towards the moon, that Basher was almost upon them before he noticed his approach. Basher, looking his ugliest and most dangerous.

Figgy acted instantly and seized Lavinia's hand.

'Quick!' he said. 'Before they start the ride.'

For some minutes the Ferris wheel had been moving a few feet then stopping to allow passengers to alight and new ones to take their place. As Figgy hurried Lavinia to the entrance, they found they were just in time to clamber into the last seats before the ride began. To the stately notes of 'The Blue Danube' they rose high above the din and bustle of the fairground until, at the highest point, they seemed to look down on a miniature world of fairy lights and models. Then they were descending, back to the hubbub below, where friends waved to friends having rides and cheered them as they swooped up towards the stars again. Nobody cheered or waved to Lavinia and Figgy. Peter was busy showing off his skill with darts, and Mr and Mrs Figg had their feet up round the television. Only Basher stood there, watching them sail by. When they came down for the third time, Lavinia noticed him.

'There's that boy,' she said.

'I know,' said Figgy.

Again and again, the wheel brought them down to earth, and there was Basher waiting. Soon the wheel would bring them down for the last time, and off they'd have to get.

When the wheel did stop, Figgy and Lavinia had just reached the top, and the chair they sat in rocked gently until with a little jerk it moved them down a few more feet to let other joy-riders climb out. So, stage by stage, they were lowered to the waiting Basher. Basher, who waited patiently, confident that he had got them.

'Have we got enough money for another go?' asked Figgy.

Lavinia shook her head.

'Not even for me?' said Figgy. 'I mean, it's me he wants.'

'No,' said Lavinia. 'There's only 10p left.'

'Oh, blimey!' Figgy said.

And then they were down, and the man who ran the Ferris wheel was hurrying them along.

Basher stood there and barred Figgy's way.

''Ere, I want you!'

'What for?' asked Figgy, weakly.

'You know what for, you rotten squealer!'

'Go away,' Lavinia said. 'We don't want to talk to you.'

'Mind your own business, Lav!' snapped Basher. 'I'm gonna get your little boyfriend here.'

'That's not fair,' said Lavinia. 'You're much bigger than he is.'

'Everyone's bigger than he is, the little squirt! But his mouth's too big and I'm gonna shut it for him!'

Figgy did the only thing he could do. He twisted round and ran, dodging past people, diving through gaps between the stalls, running without a backward glance. Had he paused, he would have seen no sign of Basher in pursuit. And what he did not see in his wild flight from the Ferris wheel was Basher lunging after him and Lavinia sticking out her foot to bring the bully down. What the onlookers saw next was talked about in Kirkston for many weeks to come.

Basher scrambled to his feet, cursing horribly, and swung a booted foot. Lavinia neatly side-stepped, caught the heel of Basher's boot and carried it up higher until Basher over-balanced and fell full-length on his back. Surprised and winded, he lay a few moments panting on the ground. Then, with greater caution, he got to his feet and squared up to Lavinia. He would not risk the boot this time, but aimed a savage blow at his opponent's nose. By swaying to her left, Lavinia avoided Basher's fist; at the same time, she grasped his arm, rolled over backwards, and — as if by magic — Basher somersaulted through the air, and once again was sprawling, helpless, in the dust. Another of Lavinia's accomplishments was her expertise in judo!

To the laughs and jeers of spectators, Basher once more struggled to his feet, but, before he could attack again, he was grabbed by his collar and the seat of his trousers. Lavinia had a champion. Peter had returned just in time to witness Lavinia's triumph.

'All right, sunshine,' he growled at Basher. 'Push off! Before she does some damage!'

Almost snivelling, Basher scuffed a sleeve across his face and slunk away into the crowd.

'And what was all that about?' asked Peter. 'Blimey! You know how to handle yourself, Lavinia, and that's for sure. You ought to have been a boy, you really ought!'

And Lavinia, who until this moment had remained perfectly cool, burst into tears.

'What did I say, Tracey? What did I say?' Peter appealed to the girl with bright green hair.

It was a silent party that trod the homeward journey. Figgy was sure that Mrs Figg must by now have found the note; Peter worried about what would happen if his parents learned that he had left the other two and

Lavinia had got into a fight; and Lavinia herself? —
Who could guess what thoughts occupied her mind?

'Lavinia,' Peter said, 'I think, perhaps, we shouldn't
mention all that to Mum and Dad — they'd only
worry, and there's no harm done is there, really?'

Mr and Mrs Figg gave them a great welcome.

'Had a lovely time? Supper's ready. Just boil the
kettle and we can make a start.'

There was no mention of the note, no hint even of
matters to be dealt with when Lavinia had gone. Figgy
noticed Peter was glancing curiously at his mother,
clearly disappointed that his plan appeared to have
misfired. Lavinia had recovered from her fit of
weeping, and, if she were somewhat less talkative than
usual, her aunt and uncle did not notice. There was
celebration trifle and a birthday cake, flickering with
twelve candles, which Lavinia blew out with one
breath, of course.

And so the last day of Lavinia's visit ended. Figgy
wriggled down into the sleeping-bag, happy in the
thought that tomorrow night he would be back in his
own room.

"Ere, Mike,' said Peter. 'Did you find that note?'

'Note? . . . Oh, *that* note. Forget about it, faceache!'

It was all bluff, naturally, but he wasn't going to let
Peter see there was still anything to worry over.

9
Quits

Lavinia was to catch a train in the early afternoon, so there was one more morning of her about the house. She helped Mrs Figg by folding the washing as she ironed it and carrying it to the linen cupboard. Mrs Figg had just begun to iron a pair of Figgy's jeans, when she stopped and fished something from the pocket.

'What's that, Mum?' asked Peter eagerly, catching Figgy's eye.

This was it! No chance of escape! And Peter *had* given him a clue: his troubles were, indeed, 'coming out in the wash'. Peter had hidden the note in a pair of Figgy's dirty jeans, just where Mum was sure to find it.

'You must have forgotten to go through all the pockets before you put them in the machine, Lavinia,' laughed Mrs Figg. 'Goodness knows what this was! It's just a bit of wood-pulp now.'

'Oh, I am sorry, Michael,' said Lavinia. 'I hope it wasn't anything important.'

'No, don't worry,' Figgy said. 'I can't think what it was.'

Lavinia was gone!

The family stood on the station platform and waved until her train disappeared into the tunnel.

'What a nice girl! What a really nice girl!' said Mrs Figg. 'Mind you, it's a bit of a strain living with perfection — but a nice change from our two!'

'I'm going out on my bike,' Peter said when they got home. 'Are my white jeans ironed, Mum?'

'Yes, sir,' said Mrs Figg. 'Upstairs in the usual place.'

And Peter hurried off to prepare himself to charm the greenhaired Tracey.

A sparkling thought set all the cells in Figgy's brain jigging with delight. It was brilliant; it was simple. It would wound Peter just where it would hurt him most — his vanity — and it would serve him right! But, if he was going to do it, he must do it now, at once!

Peter, bronzed, muscular, resplendent in white jeans, and smiling like an advertisement for toothpaste, spun downhill on his glittering bicycle to the admiring flock of girls.

'Hi!' he greeted them, and swung lightly from the saddle.

'Ugh!' Tracey cried. 'What's that?'

She pointed to an area of his trousers which filled Peter with dismay, and he felt desperately for the zip. Relief! That was secure enough... but between his legs he found thick black, sticky smears which stained his fingers when he touched them.

'What the...!' he exclaimed. Then he examined his saddle and discovered its leather sides coated with black shoe polish!

At the other end of town, Figgy hurried to the bus station. It was the fortieth time he had run away from home.